Sliding on the Edge

This story is for all the Shawnas and all the Kays who cope with deep emotional wounds.

Sliding on the Edge

C. Lee McKenzie

WestSide Books

Published by WestSide Books
60 Industrial Road
Lodi, NJ 07644
973-458-0485
Fax: 973-458-5289

Library of Congress Control Number: 2008911809

International Standard Book Number: 978-1-934813-06-5
School Edition ISBN: 978-1-934813-22-5
Cover illustration copyright © by Michael Morgenstern
Cover design by Chinedum Chukwu
Interior design by David Lemanowicz

Printed in the United States of America
10 9 8 7 6 5 4 3 2 1

First Edition

Sliding on the Edge

Chapter 1

Shawna

Something's wrong. It's not a heart-grabbing noise like when somebody jiggles the doorknob to see if it's locked. It's not a bitter smell like the electrical short we had last month, when all the breakers popped. No. It's something in the air, something like a ghost making its way through the room. And it can't be Monster, not after last night.

I squint into the morning light, then roll onto my back and blink at the damp veins in the ceiling. The toilet in the apartment above us flushes twenty-four seven. There must be ten people living up there, and our ceiling takes the brunt of 4B's high-density living.

The air conditioner isn't humming. Is that what woke me up?

My hair is plastered to the side of my face. I paid the electric bill. I'm sure I did.

Did I?

The hands on our wall clock *chunk, chunk* around to eleven. I pull on my jeans and my bra, then dig under the roll-away and haul out the rest of my clothes from yesterday. Mom's bedroom door is closed like always, so I tap on it and wait. When she doesn't yell at me to go away, I knock again, harder. Then I twist the knob and push. It's usually locked, but today it swings open.

The sheets twisted together in a heap on the bed look like they've killed each other. The dresser drawers stick out like stair steps, their insides scooped clean. I pull the door shut and roll my forehead back and forth against the peeling paint. I'm in free-fall, clutching at clouds.

Four steps across the hall and I'm in the bathroom. It's been stripped. The clutter of Mom's bottles and sprays, mascara tubes, and nail polish, all gone. My toothbrush and a crushed, half-empty toothpaste tube curled up on the back of the toilet make a lonely still life.

I splash my face with cold water, then lean against the sink and hold on with both hands. More than anything, I wish I could crawl in and swizzle down the drain along with the water.

What's she up to this time?

The face in the mirror doesn't have a clue.

In the kitchen the sink full of take-out containers is losing its battle to mold. We've lived here three months, a record. The mold, on the other hand, was a tenant before we paid our first rent check. It has been around so long, it's immune to bleach. I gave up after the first week.

A folded piece of paper sticks out from under the greasy skillet. When I tug at it, a bus ticket and a hundred-dollar bill flutter onto the linoleum floor. *Where did she get a hundred? . . . And how? . . . damn.* I kneel and scoop up the money, then stare at the piece of paper next to it. At the top is Casino Royale's logo, which has showgirls playing cards and roulette wheels down the side. Royale is one of her favorite gambling places, one I can usually stake out at about six in the morning when I need to get lunch money from her. There's a note on the piece of paper, but I don't pick it up. I don't want to touch it and I don't want to read it.

The clock keeps *chunking*. My knees go numb. Upstairs 4B's toilet flushes. I turn my head so her words aren't sideways.

She starts with "Shawna sweetie, Dylan and me are going to New Jersey to try our luck at some other tables."

Huh? I squeeze my eyes shut then open them. There's more. I pick up the paper and get off my knees.

"He bot you a tiket to California and left you a hundred (he's a sweet heart, right?). Your granma lives in a place called sweet river. Its close to sacramento in California. Go there so I can get in touch once were settled, hon.

Jackie"

In the bottom corner of the paper Mom scribbled something else, but while her writing is hard to make out, her scribbling takes code-breaker training. I don't bother to try.

Instead, I read the note one more time and turn it over, in case she added more on the back. Like, "I'll miss you."

No. The back is blank.

I hang over, resting my head on my knees. *Don't get the shakes. Don't get the shakes. You know what happens when you get the shakes.*

I wish I could be five again . . . I wish she would prop me up on pillows like she did then, and feed me ice cream . . . and I would lick the spoon and she would laugh and I would laugh and she wouldn't leave until I slept.

Blood is backing up behind my eyeballs. I need oxygen, quick. I straighten up and walk to the air conditioner, giving it a hard smack on the side. The blades inside crank over and cool air fans across my face. I stand there, thinking about my mom, writing the note while I was asleep, leaving without saying something.

Like "Good-bye."

"See ya."

"Be careful."

And I know Dylan watched her write that note. She never calls herself Mom when he's around.

Finally, I study the tight scribble in the bottom corner. "Kay Stone" and a phone number. Below that is, "ps you gotta sneak out of the apartment. Rents over do."

"Oh, man, not again." My voice sounds whiney—like I'm six, not sixteen.

On the calendar hanging over the hot plate, I'd scrawled "rent due" in purple marker across the first week. The rent was due last Saturday, so I figure I have about an hour before Tuan bangs on the door.

I gotta lie down.

Gotta think.

I sprawl across the roll-away and bury my head under my pillow. Mom could come up with doozies, but this one is pretty big. She's skipped out for a few days at a time before, but she's never left me a ticket or a grandmother to go and stay with.

And what about this Kay Stone? That's a new name on the family tree. I don't remember ever hearing the name Stone.

And why should I go, anyway? I can make it on my own without some granny minding my business. It would serve Mom right if I just cashed in the ticket and stayed right here in Vegas. She'd never find me here, and I can take care of myself. Get a job.

"Screw her!"

I hurl the pillow across the room, knock over the bullet lamp, and send it crashing to the floor. *Great, now Tuan'll come pounding on the door to see what kind of damage I've done to his furniture.*

I wrap Sweetheart's hundred and the ticket inside the note and jam them into my jeans pocket. I skim my hand over the top of the fridge and reach to the back, feeling for the goods I've hidden there. The envelope is dirty and torn, so I take care to fold it over the cards inside, then slip the packet into my hip pocket. Then I find my thin treasure, one of Dylan's razor blades wrapped in toilet paper. As I pull it forward, my hand knocks over a small plastic bottle. It falls and rolls across the floor. I scoop it up. It's Mom's sleeping pills she got after a guy named Regan dumped her. Just thinking about him makes my flesh

11

creep. *Guess she doesn't need these anymore, now that she's got old Dylan.* I put the razor blade and the pills inside a paper bag.

Packed.

Now, all I have to do is escape without making Tuan suspicious, but that's not going to be easy. Sour Puss Tuan circles his apartments like a reconnaissance plane every day. My only hope is to do like Mom taught me.

"The best way to bail out on your rent," she'd say, "is to act totally normal."

So I bounce down the stairs like always, and check my expression in the mirror outside Tuan's apartment door. On it is a tag fluttering from a piece of string: "For Sale/$2." Tuan's been trying to sell that cracked glass since we moved in. If I stand so the crack cuts my face into two pieces, I actually look kinda interesting. If I stand on one side and get my full face, I just look dorky. No sixteen-year-old looks like me in Vegas, except for the Keno players' kids from Kansas.

"Somebody's got to be able to work a regular job. And that's gotta be you," Mom would say, jabbing her finger into my chest.

Once a month, sometimes twice, like in the summer when school's out—that's as regular as it gets with Mom and me—I play a lost teen, asking for directions at the casino door while Mom lifts tourist wallets, and, I have to say, she's pretty good. We've never been busted. A couple of close calls, but the cops have never booked her.

The door opens and I jump at Tuan's sudden appearance. He's armed with the paintbrush that I see him use every day to cover up graffiti. We live way too close to Morrie's Hardware, and all the taggers test their Krylon spray nozzles on our wall before they head for their real targets downtown.

"Good morning, Tuan." I smile and smooth my hair in his mirror like I'm in no hurry to go anyplace. His eyes don't blink. He's kinda snaky that way.

"Not good," he grumbles.

He jerks his door closed behind him and stomps outside. I follow and watch while he swipes gray paint over the red-and-black stucco art.

"Las Vegas!" He spits into the gutter. "Hoodlums do this. All time."

While he dunks his brush into the paint I slip past him. I want to run, but I make myself walk the way the girls do on the street when they're working. "Look at us," they say. "We're not doing anything wrong, just walking." *Come on, Tuan, watch me leave like I'm coming back, like this is the same as any day since I moved into your dump.* I almost make the corner when he yells.

"You betta tell her rent due at noon or you both out!" He flings his arm, and paint flies like gray raindrops onto the sidewalk.

I wave and smile.

When I reach the corner, I can still feel his snaky eyes on my back.

Chapter 2

Shawna

There are lots of good things about Las Vegas, but the best thing is it never shuts down. If I steer clear of the old section of town and the back alleys, moving from casino to casino, looking bored like I'm waiting for my parents, I can stay pretty safe around the clock. The trick is to avoid crossing paths with the same security guards too often. I'm thinking that if I hang around Vegas, I can make it on my own. Have before. *Yeah. Sure I can.*

I've been knocking around town since I left my buddy Tuan this morning. It's now four in the afternoon. I'm starved and it's time to make some life decisions. I know Kibby's Hamburgers is hiring, but nobody works long at Kibby's. Their last burger-flipper, who sat next to me in biology, filled me in on the night manager who grew extra hands whenever she was alone with him. That picture I get in my mind makes me shiver. So I'll check out Stan's Café. They hire a lot.

When I get to the café, there isn't a HELP WANTED sign in the window. I walk inside anyway. Stan's fries are still fifty cents—within my budget—and I order one grease-soaked box of limp potatoes. With a plop of ketchup for color, I'm in heaven. Today's newspaper is on an empty table, so with my lunch or dinner—I haven't decided which one—I shuffle through the pages to the help wanted ads.

"Wanted:

Part-time fry cook. Experience Required."

I can fry stuff.

$8.00/hr. Midnight to four A.M. Pete's Dugout.

That's down on Pioneer. Not where I want to work.

Housekeeping $6.50/hr. Motel Escondido.

Hmmm. Toilets. Maybe not.

I'm down to my last fry and still hungry. That hundred Mom left has to last until I land a job or . . . I pull the note out and read it again. "Your granma lives in a place called sweet river."

What are my options? Stay here, quit school, and get a job cleaning toilets or call the number on Mom's note. I lay my head on the grease-flecked newspaper and listen to the paper crinkle under my ear. *Wanted: under-educated sixteen-year-old to scrape crud off the floor. Experience Required.*

My stomach growls.

"You sick or somethin'?"

I jerk upright to face the guy standing over me.

"Ahh, no. Just tired."

"Go sleep someplace else. This is a restaurant, not a flophouse."

"You could'a fooled me." I grab my paper bag off the

table and head for the door. He is one big scowl and I'm
not going toe to toe with a greasy grump. Outside, I poke
my head back in, flip him off, and yell, "I'm going to the
emergency room. Your grease is rancid, Pedro!"

He's after me in a shot, and around the corner I slip
into the nearest store before he can see me. He does a fast
waddle past the window while I peek from behind a dress
rack.

"May I help you?" A sales girl peers over a 25% off
sign at the end of the clothes rack.

*Gee, sure, yes. Please help me find my mother, okay?
She's somewhere in New Jersey at a crap table. There'll be
a sleazy guy with blond hair next to her.* "I don't think so."

"Are you looking for anything special?"

*Actually, I am. Some answers would be nice for a
start. Maybe a life if you got one of those in here.* "No." I
clutch my paper bag and the pills rattle inside their plastic
bottle. "Just looking." *Just searching for a way out.*

She smiles and moves to another customer.

My stomach is flipping pancakes, and I feel like hurling. I squint my eyes and swallow. Maybe the grease was
rancid after all. Or maybe that part of my anatomy can't
stand the idea I've got circulating through my brain: A
place called Sweet River.

"Are you okay?" It's the chirpy sales girl again, her
face curious and a bit worried.

When I look past her into the mirror I can see why
she's looking at me that way. I've turned the color of paste.
"I think I got some bad food."

Now her face is more than worried. She's already seeing a big mess, one she'll get stuck having to clean up.

The greasy grump walks past, back to his "restaurant." He could have been my next employer. Oh man. I make my decision. I'm trying the granny package.

After breaking the hundred for change, I step into the bus depot phone booth. I pick up the receiver and punch in the first ten numbers. But when I get to the last digit, my finger freezes midair. What if—I glance at the name again—Kay Stone doesn't answer? I know my job options in this town, and I can't go back to Tuan's, that's for sure. He's already changed the locks by now, and anything I left is in his back room. It'll sit there until some poor desperate sap needs something like our aluminum pot and pays him five bucks for it like we did. I punch the last number on the phone pad and wait.

One ring.

Two.

"Hello." A woman's voice is on the other end of the phone, but it doesn't sound like a grandmother. It isn't creaky or wispy. It sounds like it belongs to someone a lot younger. *Oh, no. Mom gave me a wrong number.*

"Uhh. Is . . . uh . . . this Kay Stone?"

"Yes."

"Well—" I hadn't thought exactly how I'd say this next part, but now there isn't any time to choose my words. "My name's Shawna. I'm sixteen and my mom says you're my grandmother."

The phone goes silent.

"Are you there?" I can't risk her hanging up because all I have is Sweetheart's hundred, and I'm using a chunk of it on this call.

17

I can barely hear her breathing. I hope she isn't having a heart attack.

"Yes." Finally. A reply all the way from Sweet River.

"Well, here's the deal. My mom's split and she left me this ticket to Sacramento. She said to call you and let you know." I wait through another long dead silence. "I hate to rush you, but I'm running out of money on this call and—"

"What's your mother's name?"

"Jackie."

"Your father?"

Oh damn. Mom told me once, but she'd been in her "I-don't-want-to-talk-about-it" mood, so even though I hadn't been sure what she'd said, I'd dropped it.

"I think it was Nic or Rick. He's dead." I hear her swallow. Is she drinking something? I don't think she's buying that I'm telling the truth. "Hello?"

"When does your bus arrive in Sacramento?"

I check the schedule I'd picked up. "About ten tomorrow morning."

Another long silence. *These pauses are killing me.*

"What do you look like, so I can find you at the station?" she finally asks.

I almost say, "Dorky," but instead I say, "I've got black hair and brown eyes. I'm about five-four, and I'm wearing a T-shirt with—" I pull the shirt front out and check to see which one I have on, "*Bad Ass Attitude,*" I say.

She clears her throat. "I'll meet you at the bus station . . . Shawna."

I hang up knowing that at least she remembered my name.

The phone booth smells like pee, and I'm glad to escape into the bus terminal where Lysol rules.

"That went well, don't you think?" I say to no one, just to reassure myself.

A scruffy guy sleeping on a bench opens his eyes to slits and peers up at me.

"I'm not talking to you."

"Then put an egg in your shoe and beat it," he slurs through yellow teeth.

I have an hour before the bus leaves and I'm hungry, so I grab a hot dog and smear it with mustard and ketchup. It's a long trip to Sacramento, and I need more in my stomach than French fries before I get on the bus. I stash a handful of ketchup packets in my paper bag too. Mom and I lived on ketchup soup for a week once, before she came up with our lost kid act. Call me crazy, but once in a while I crave some good old homemade ketchup soup.

As I stuff the last of the hot dog into my mouth, it occurs to me that I should have asked Kay Stone one question. Was she Jackie's mother or my father's?

19

Chapter 3

Kay

Kay dropped the phone onto the cradle and stared out the kitchen window. Everything outside looked just as it had a few minutes ago. The horses grazed on the hillside. Kenny leaned into the gray mare and held her hoof in his knobby hand while he scraped thrush from under her shoe. Buster was doing canine yoga, rooting out the burrs from his bushy tail and scratching behind his ears for the fleas that even sheep dip couldn't kill.

But now nothing was the same.

As Kay sank onto the chair, she grasped the corner of the kitchen table. Once settled, she cradled her head in her hands.

Sixteen years. Such a long time, and no time at all.

The voice on the phone sounded so young—and so . . . hard. Could she believe what the girl had said? There were scams all the time to dupe the unsuspecting out of their money. She'd worked too hard to lose everything to some con artist. By the end of the year, she figured, she'd be out of debt—if none of the boarders left, if none of her horses got colicky, if, if, if. . . .

By now her coffee was cold. She walked to the sink and poured it out. By tomorrow she had to decide what to do. That wasn't very much time. She needed to talk to Kenny.

She pushed open the screen door, walked down the porch steps, and strode toward the barn. How many times had she traveled this distance, calling to Kenny Fargo? More than she cared to count. He'd always been there—in a stall, gentling a horse under his hands; in the tack room, putting things to order; or in his trailer. He'd been the one constant in her life, and kept her going when everyone else vanished.

So once again she was trudging out to talk to the man who knew horses and good whiskey, and so very much more. As Kenny led her gray mare into the barn, she caught up and stroked her favorite horse's neck. The gray turned to nuzzle her hair. Even as upside-down as she felt following that phone call, the warm animal breath made her feel calm.

"Something's happened," she said.

Kenny closed the mare's stall door and faced her. "From your look this is going to take some time." He pulled a plug of tobacco from his shirt pocket and sat on the bench alongside the wall. He heard her out, as usual staying quiet while she spoke.

"She sounded . . . scared. Why is she calling me now, after so many years, after I'd finally stopped trying to find her? What's Jackie up to this time?" Kay shook her head. "I don't know if I can believe she's who she says she is. She is the right age, if she's telling the truth about that. But what if it's a scam? What if she got my name from a . . . a mailing label in the garbage or—" Kay didn't know where con artists stole information about their victims, but this could be what was going on. "But if that were it, then how would she know Jackie's name?" Kay turned on her heels in sudden anger. "Then again, why wouldn't she know her own father's name?"

"Seems like you're asking a lot of questions," Kenny said, biting off a chunk of tobacco. He chewed slowly and let silence hang between them. The horses shuffled in their stalls, and Buster circled until he found just the right spot that fit his body, then he curled head to fluffy tail. "Also seems like you're bent on finding the answers."

He was right. She already knew she had to meet the bus in the morning. She had to see this girl. Talk to her. Why had she doubted that she would? She'd had no choice from the minute she'd heard the words, "You're my grand-mother."

Chapter 4

Kay

A little before ten the next morning, Kay pulled to the curb across the street from the bus depot. She climbed from the cab and leaned against her truck, a veteran horse ranch vehicle. Its dents and scrapes screamed, "Look out! Uninsured vehicle coming through." She liked it that way. This nothing-left-to-lose truck summed her up well, and always got her the right of way.

The ten o'clock bus rolled to a stop, then the door wheezed open.

Kay chewed her bottom lip. She felt dampness under her arms and wiped her palms on her jeans. She hadn't had the jitters for so long that the signals her body was sending felt foreign, yet they called back other times she'd been on edge. Like, the day she and Peter were married, and her dress took a bath in sweat. She was not the sweet scented bride of her dreams by the time she'd wobbled down the aisle on those white satin pumps. So many other things went wrong that day, she'd blocked out the rest of her memories. From when she'd started to sneeze after "I do," to the end of the reception, it was all pretty much forgotten.

Why was she thinking about her wedding, anyway? What had that memory to do with today? She closed her eyes and willed her heart to stop hurling itself against her ribs.

Simmer down. You're not stepping into a minefield, she thought. You're meeting a young girl who might be your granddaughter.

Minefield.

She regretted that metaphor as soon as it flitted into her mind. It set off the slide show she couldn't stop: *Click.* Herself, gripping the letter. *Click.* The two men standing at the door, jaws squared, faces set. *Click.* Peter leaning forward in his armchair, his head cradled in his hands.

Kay pressed her palms against her closed eyes, pushing back the sudden sting of old tears.

She glanced up at the sound of the bus pulling away. A lone girl stood looking around, like a visitor from another planet.

Well, Kay thought, *Sacramento and Las Vegas are different planets. Those bus depots with slot machines at every door look alien to me.*

Kay took a moment to see the downtown from a stranger's point of view. The clatter of cars and busses filled the air, their exhausts belching fumes. Several blocks away, the gold ball atop the state capitol building poked up from behind the jagged ridge of office roofs. This part of the city was built sometime in the nineteen forties or fifties. Many of the storefronts were a faded turquoise or imitation stone that Peter had called "Late Tacky." Hand-written signs promising the best for less looked like super-sized Band-Aids on the grimy windows.

Kay studied the dark-haired girl across the street. Dressed in a T-shirt and low-cut jeans, she clutched a brown paper bag. Like most of the girls these days, she looked a little sloppy and a lot sassy. Kay tried to read her expression. *Some apprehension*, she thought. *That's normal. She's in a strange place about to meet someone for the first time. But what else is there?*

The girl leaned against the wall of the depot. She looked up then down the street, as if deciding which way to go if that grandmother didn't arrive.

What are her options? Kay wondered. *What if I don't cross the street, tell her who I am? Where will she go? What will happen to her?* She ran down the list of strays she'd taken in over the years: Buster, who'd limped in on three legs with a deep cut in his front paw. Kenny, with a suffering man's eyes. The uncountable cats. Two donkeys. All unwanted or abused, until they landed on her back porch.

She looked again at the girl with the brown paper bag. Under the tight jeans and tough expression was another stray needing a safe place to stay.

Kay stepped into the street and walked toward Shawna.

Chapter 5

Shawna

How come nobody ever told me Northern California could be cold in August?

When I changed buses in Stockton, I shivered so much that people around me must have thought I had malaria. It turned out good though, because nobody sat next to me on the bus. I stretched out and dozed off, wondering if I left Monster in Vegas, wondering if Monster can travel. If he can't he'll have to find somebody else to push around. But what will I do if he doesn't show up anymore? Is that pathetic or what? You get one secret bud and his name is Monster.

What a relief to step off in Sacramento, where at ten in the morning, it's already in the nineties—almost like back home. But this sure isn't Vegas, and I'm feeling all jumpy inside. *What if Kay Stone decides she doesn't want to meet me? All I got is three twenties, two tens, and some change. There's no way I can get back to Vegas. And even if there was, what would I do when I got there? Damn.*

I lean against the wall by the front doors of the bus depot and count backwards from one hundred, an old habit from waiting on Mom.

"Shawna?"

I look up at the woman coming toward me. I try to find something familiar about her. Maybe her eyes or her hair look like Mom's. She's tall, but otherwise there's nothing of my mother there.

"You're not what I expected, either," she says like she's reading my mind. "Where are your suitcases?"

I hold up my paper bag.

"We can get you some clothes later." She turns and walks back across the street.

So, is she taking me home with her?

She looks over her shoulder. "Coming?"

I shrug. *Guess that means yes.* I step off the curb into the street. She walks with wide swinging steps in mud-caked boots. Every step or so, clumps of dirt come free and scatter across the sidewalk. Her jeans fit snugly over her long legs, and I'm having trouble imagining her as anyone's grandmother.

She stops at a black pickup that looks like it runs into everything it gets near.

"Door's open," she says. "Climb in."

The battered door screeches when I open it, like it doesn't want me inside.

She starts the engine and releases the brake. "Seat belt."

And that is the last she speaks for the hour we drive together. I'm used to Mom's chatter, so sitting beside Kay

27

Stone, who is living up to her last name, makes me chew my thumbnail to a stub. I wonder if she's ever going to talk to me again.

The sign for Sweet River comes and goes before I blink. *Is it a ghost town?* We wind around up a mountain, cross a couple of bridges, and turn onto a dirt road that looks like a dry creek bed. That's when the truck turns ugly and slams my head on the roof. I grab the seat and hold on.

On either side of us, horses stretch their long necks through wood fence rails and yank up grass almost out of reach. I count three scruffy critters standing near the road, all taking a siesta. *Could those things be donkeys?*

Kay stops at a row of mailboxes and grabs a handful of letters.

"Mostly bills," she says, tossing them on the seat between us.

I jump at the sudden sound of her voice, but she doesn't seem to notice that I've practically left my skin.

She pulls to a stop in time to save my teeth from coming loose and falling into my lap. We're in front of a dark red house with white trim that looks like a squat version of the barn a hundred yards or so behind it. A cluster of trees shades the truck and I look up, wondering what happens when one of those suckers falls. I'm not used to trees that big. They look like they might reach down to nab me by the back of the neck when I walk underneath. In Vegas big trees are edged in blinking neon. Guys hose the dust off and change the bulbs. I'd like to see anyone try to dust one of these giant mutants. There's a fenced area in front of the house with three naked sheep nosing the grass while a white, ragged-looking dog roams behind their bare back-sides. The dog, tongue out in a summer pant, turns to look at us, then trots over and thumps his tail against Kay's leg when she steps out of the truck.

Kay strokes his head and he wags his tail so hard, his whole body sways side to side. "This is Buster. Buster, Shawna."

A man sitting on the front porch waves, sets aside his newspaper, and comes down the steps. His knees point in opposite directions, and his legs form an arch big enough for a Volkswagen to drive through.

"That's Kenny. He works for me." Kay slams the cab door.

"This her?" The old man spits to the side and wipes his mouth with the back of his hand.

"Yep," she says.

"You got suitcases to carry inside?" he asks.

"No. She travels light. Come on inside, Shawna. Are you hungry?"

I shrug.

Her lips pull up tight in a bundle and she gives me a look.

What did I do? What didn't I do?

"Well, let's go see what we've got anyway," she says.

Inside, the house is cool, but I can tell by the way it feels that she doesn't have air conditioning. By two, the furniture is going to melt in this place. Even Tuan's dump had air, well, it did most of the time. But this house is way bigger than anything I've lived in besides the Casino Royale, which I kind of consider mine because I eat there a lot and use the restrooms—those marble columns and gold faucets are the best.

"You want a ham sandwich?" Kay stands in front of the open fridge.

I shrug. "I guess."

"Milk?"

I shrug.

She turns and, uh-oh, she's bunched her lips again.

"Do me a favor. Don't shrug all the time, like nothing matters."

"Sure," I say, before I realize my shoulders are heading north to my ears.

Man, having a grandmother is way different than I'd imagined. Come to think of it, I never did imagine a grandmother. I'd thought about having a dog once, but Tuan told me he'd eat it if I brought one into his apartments. That's something else I never imagined, eating a dog. Gag.

But now that I study her face, I'm thinking maybe that would be easier than getting used to living with a grandmother like this one. It's kind of like getting a computer or software without a manual, you know?

Chapter 6

Shawna

I'm concentrating on keeping my shoulders still. When I shrug it makes Granny go sour, and I don't want her pissed from the get-go. Since she hasn't handed me a user's manual, I've decided to make one up. Entry #1 under Getting Started: No Shrugging.

Kay gives me a quick tour of her place and lets me wash up. I'm not used to so many rooms. I'm thinking I need a map, but I find my way back to the kitchen and sit at the table. I know I'm in a way different world already because the legs on this table are even. I don't have to stick a matchbook under one to keep the milk from sloshing over.

I chew on a ham sandwich while Kay and Kenny talk about things I've never heard of before, like tacks and soapy saddles.

I can tell the two of them are close. Every once in a while, when Kay is going on about some horse, the old man's eyes go kind of soft. He loves my grandmother, I'm pretty sure. But I can tell it's a one-way street. Everything about Kay is business—no mushy center in 'ole Grandma.

She's not an easy mark for a con, either. Mom would have waited for someone else to come along before giving me the signal to go into my lost kid act. Mom was the expert at sizing up chumps, but even I can tell Grandma isn't one of them. She's got a sharp look about her. And I'm going to have to be very careful about what I do and say around her. That should go in the manual, Entry #2: Do Not Try to Con.

"I best get back to work," Kenny says. "I've gotta check on your mare."

"Is her temp up again?" Kay asks quickly, and her voice is tight.

"A little, but I'm keeping an eye on her." He walks out the back door and spits over the railing.

"I've got chores, too." Kay clears the table and sets the dishes in the sink. "Get some rest or do whatever you want. You know where the food is, so help yourself. There are books in there." She points toward her office at the end of the hall that she'd showed me when she gave me the tour.

"You got a TV?" I ask.

She doesn't look at me. She grabs a wide-brimmed straw hat off a hook by the kitchen door and walks out.

"Guess that means no." *No MTV, no shopping channels? What does she expect me to do for the rest of my life? Watch Kenny spit brown juice all day?* "Arrrg!"

I roam through the house again, like I did when I followed Kay and she showed me where I'd bunk. All of her rooms look about the same—big, with dark beams like square bones holding up the ceilings, and cowhides stretched across the walls. She's got her own style, that's for sure. And *glitzy* is not a word in her decorating vocabulary. I poke my head into her office, a room bigger than our whole apartment in Vegas. Kay's super-sized desk is piled with stacks of folders and sits in the middle of the room—Command Central. I step inside. Walls covered with bookshelves rise up around me like a canyon. For a minute I feel like I've taken a wrong turn and wound up at a bookstore or a library. It feels weird to see so many books in a room down the hall from the kitchen or the bathroom—not like where I've ever lived before.

I walk past the shelves and run my finger across the spines, something I can usually only do at the library. There's everything about horses, presidents, history, and poetry. And that's just what's at eye level. I can't see what's overhead.

Mom only reads the jokes on bar napkins. Entry #3: Granny's Not Dumb. Living with her is going to take some getting used to.

Down the hall is *my room*. I step inside and close the door.

I've never had a room with a door. Mom always took the bedroom and I got the sofa or the cot. Or, like at Tuan's, the roll-away. I open the door and close it again—just because I can. The closet is empty. The dresser drawers are too. But there's a smell . . . leather and spice, and not girly. Some guy must have lived in here once. On each side of the big bed are nightstands stacked with . . . more books and tall brass lamps. I feel like I've landed in heaven. There are books everywhere I look. A picture of a

33

wild-haired man with deep-set eyes and bushy brows as thick as his mustache stares up from a book cover. I recognize Mark Twain's face from the English class I was in for a few weeks last year. My teacher read a lot of his stuff out loud.

I pick up the Twain book and leaf through its pages. The book falls open to a page with a corner folded down. Someone underlined a sentence halfway down: *Pity is for the living, envy is for the dead.* I read it a couple of times, soaking up the idea. *Wow! Who was the depresso with the pen?*

I put the book down and turn to explore the rest of my space.

Green plaid curtains hang on each side of a wide window that looks out on Kay's barn and the hillside where horses nose the grass. Some of them have moved to the shade of a wide-branched tree, where they huddle like they're having some kind of meeting. Way past Kay's barn, and on the other side of her fence, is a small shack. It leans to one side, and its roof buckles in the center, ready to crumble in on itself. One good push and that place goes splat. On one side of the wobbly place sits a square block foundation. And at one end, steps lead from a weedy brick path up to an empty door frame. It's the only upright part of what looks like it used to be a house. At the back of that falling-to-pieces property stands a tacky-looking gray barn. It shows no signs of paint and has lots of missing boards. Three horses line up alongside the shady barn wall—a black one, a spotted brown and white, and a gray with a deep swayback. The black one stands taller than the rest, but even from this far, I can see they're a sad-looking bunch. Their heads droop like it's too hard to hold them up, and their ribs show along their sides. None look as good as Kay's. Hers are shiny and fleshy, with long tight muscles hugged close by their skin. Any guy would be happy to strut around with pecs like the ones on those horses.

Kenny walks out of Kay's barn. He holds his fingers to his mouth and whistles so loud I can hear him from inside the house, even with the windows shut. A reddish-brown horse gallops out from under the shade tree and stops in front of the old man. The horse lowers its head. Kenny steps onto a fallen log and in one swing sits on the horse's bare back. Now I understand why his legs form an arch. They're the exact shape of a horse. Together they shoot out of sight—Old Spit on the range.

I pull the bottle of Mom's sleeping pills and the ratty envelope out of the paper bag. The lamp table has a drawer, so I stuff the pills in the back and tuck the thin blade wrapped in toilet paper under the bottle. I sit on the edge of the bed and take out my stack of old library cards from the envelope. Dealing them like a poker hand, I spread them across the quilt. This is a map of where I've lived: Houston, L.A, Barstow, Bakersfield, Reno. Ah, yes, Reno. That's where the gambling bug bit Mom, and from then on, there wasn't a casino she didn't love. That's how we wound up in Las Vegas.

The loud knock on the door shoots me upright. For a minute I'm back in Vegas, ready to face Tuan with his hand out for the rent.

"Shawna?" It's Kay.

I wait, but when she doesn't open the door, I get up and let her in.

"Come on. Kenny says you'll need some pocket money when school starts, so he'll put you on salary."

"On salary. That means work, right?"

"You got it."

"What kind?" I back against the wall and put my foot on it to brace myself.

She does one of those long blinks that flash *fed up*. "On a horse ranch we work with horses. Does that surprise you?"

"I don't work with horses." I want that clear, so I might as well lay it out right up front.

"I see." She leans against the open door. "Maybe you mean that you've never worked with horses before now, but since you have the opportunity, you *will*."

"No. That's not what I mean. Not even close."

"That's too bad." She folds her arms across her chest and stares out the window.

"Because on this horse ranch, if you don't do your chores during the day, not only do you not get pocket money, you don't eat, either."

Now *I* fold my arms across my chest. "I guess I'll just have to call the child protective people and tell them about this."

"The phone's in my office." She walks away. "Tell Marla Perdy hello for me when you get her."

"Who?"

"Marla Perdy. She's in charge of the County Welfare

36

Agency. You know, child abuse, that sort of thing. You explain how you got here, how I'm putting you to work, and paying you. She's very understanding."

"Shit!"

"Did you say something?" Kay looks over her shoulder at me.

"No." *What's the use? I'm stuck in this happy acres horse camp until I can figure a way out.*

"So, are we going to the barn?" she asks, like I've got a choice.

Sigh. "Yes." Still I wonder what she'd do if I slammed the door and didn't budge. Would she actually kick me out?

I follow my leggy grandmother out the back door, down the steps, and across the yard toward the barn.

That one question that's been niggling around in my brain, ever since I read Mom's note, starts to niggle again. I think I should ask her now. "Hey!"

She stops and turns, fixing me with a sour look.

"Kay? Grandma?" I'm not sure what to call her, but *Hey* does not sit well, I can tell.

"Call me Kay."

"Right. Well, Kay, I was wondering about something. Like, are you Jackie's mom or my dad's mom?"

Now her expression shifts to hard, and the rest of her goes heavy. I imagine her sinking into the ground. "I'm your father's mother." She barely says the last word when she turns around and heads toward the barn again.

Hmmm. So it was her son who ditched Mom and me. Well, she doesn't want to talk about my parents. That's flat out clear, so I'll wait to ask the other question: Was his name Rick or Nic?

Chapter 7

Shawna

I'm backed against the barn wall, as far as I can get from a horse that's glaring at me. I've never been so close to anything this big and smelly before. Well, this smelly, yes, but this big, no.

Do horses eat people?

Kenny stands with one hand on each hip, his mouth working hard on a piece of what he calls *chaw*. The horse the size of a casino stands by his side.

"I hate horses. Look at this one's eyes. He feels the same about me."

"Makes no difference to me, Missy." He spits into the bushes. "You can love 'em or you can hate 'em. In either case, you are gonna learn to curry their backsides without gettin' your butt kicked. Comprende?"

"Oh, man," I groan. "I am so not a horse person."

"You'll catch on." He holds out a brush to me.

I shake my head and drag the toes of my shoes into the dirt. "No way. Look man, I came here because I had to, but I don't have to stay." I fold my arms over my chest.

He ignores me. "This here is Stud."

"I don't care if he's King Tut. I'm not touching him."

"Scared?"

"No," I shout, and the horse dances sideways. "Damn!" I jump out of the way, just in time to not get crushed against the barn wall.

Kenny hurls another arc of dark spit into his favorite bush. "Just a tad skeered?" The old fart laughs.

"Give me the damned brush."

He tosses it to me. "You just learned your first lesson, Missy. Don't yell around a critter that's four times your size. Now here's another one for you. This horse kicks like hell when you swipe his haunch in just the right spot." Kenny spits again and walks away.

"Hey! Wait up, Poncho," I shout.

He stops but doesn't turn around.

"Okay. Please wait, . . . Mr. Kenny."

"If you got any questions, the name's Kenny Fargo to you, Missy." He looks at me over his shoulder.

"All right. How in the hell do I do this . . . this curry thing without getting my ass kicked, Kenny Fargo?"

"Thought you'd never ask."

Kenny walks back to me, takes the brush from my hand and begins a slow even stroke over Stud's quivering back. "When you come to this part," he points to the horse's right hind leg, "you go real gentle. The other side don't matter. But treat this side like raw nerve." He holds the brush out to me again. "Give it a try, Missy."

"The name's Shawna." I snatch the brush out of his hand.

Stud's hindquarters don't give me nearly as much trouble as Mom's choice of boyfriends. The horse shivers under the brush as I come down his right leg, but he doesn't shy away or kick me into the side of the barn, which I half expected. Kenny watches but doesn't say anything. I decide the whole place is filled with people who don't talk much and horses that wait until your guard is down before they'd sink their teeth into your butt.

"How's that?" I ask when I've brushed a three-sixty around Stud.

"That's one." Kenny Fargo takes Stud's lead and pulls him back into his stall.

One? My arms already ache, and the old man's bringing out another horse.

Kay strides past, leading a gray horse toward the barn. Her long-legged walk matches the gray's, as though they are both the same kind of animal—one with only two legs, the other with the right number.

She looks at me, but I get the feeling she doesn't see me at all. It's like she's picturing somebody else. It creeps me out and I turn away.

Kenny Fargo leads out three more horses, one after the other, each with twitchy butts and big teeth. I do the curry thing while he *supervises*, then he puts them back in their stalls.

"How many of these do I have to curry?" I shout at his back. Kenny doesn't answer me.

He walks another horse out and hooks its leash or lead—whatever they call the thing—to a hook on the side of the barn. Then he leans back while I brush and brush

41

and brush. I've almost forgotten I'd asked him anything when he says, "All together, we got fifteen. The good news is I already done the others today, and the mules don't get curried much at all." He smiles a wide brown smile and runs his hand over the horse's side. "Looks good. I think you're getting the hang of this curry business." He leads this last horse to its stall. When he comes back, he's carrying a long pitchfork.

"Now comes the real easy part." He puts the pitchfork into my right hand. "Fresh grass hay is over there." He points to the corner in the back of the barn. "All eighteen of these beauties need a couple of flakes."

I must look blank because he says, "That's a good forkful. Then 'yer done for the night, Miss . . . Shawna."

"Where are you going?" I yell. He's already around the corner of the barn, but he ducks his head back and looks at me.

"My trailer. Got some things to do before dinner. You got a problem with that?"

"Wouldn't matter if I did." I dig the pitchfork into the pile of hay.

Okay. Mark Twain is right. Pity is for the living. I understand envying a dead guy, who doesn't have to do what I'm doing—a lifetime of currying skittery horses, forking hay, and trying to dodge Kenny Fargo's spit . . . that is pitiful. Not to mention how my arms feel. They hang at my sides like sticks pegged at the shoulders. I've carried so many of Mom's suitcases up rickety stairs and down again that I know something about being tired. But this is actual pain. And all due to those super-sized animals that don't do

42

diddly all day, except eat the hay that I have to pitch into their stalls. I've got to figure a way back to Vegas, 'cause this deal really sucks.

"I need a break." The gray in the stall next to me nods and snorts at me. "At least something around here listens," I say to her.

I walk outside, breathe in the fresh air, and exhale the smell of hay and horses. From the barn I can see the kitchen windows, with Kay passing back and forth—looking like the queen in her castle. My first dinner with Grandma: This is going to be interesting. I just hope she doesn't feed me what she feeds her horses—I've really had it with straw!

Chapter 8

Kay

In the kitchen, Kay pretended that peeling the potatoes for this dinner was like doing it any other night. She filled her big white enamel pot with cold water, then carefully peeled each tuber, sculpting it from its gritty skin. She dug out the eyes and plunged the potato into the pot, as she'd done since helping her mother cook for their ranch hands, when she'd learned about cooking first hand.

Kay believed in having regularity in her life—setting up systems that made the day run smoothly. For over sixteen years she'd managed the ranch, paying her bills and building a life she liked to think was solid and respectable. She'd never been bored with this rancher's life, and at the end of every day, she was always too tired to be bored. But she'd given up being happy when Nic died. And then, after Peter left, well, what was there to be happy about?

The back porch door slammed. Kay knew it wouldn't be Kenny. He knew better than to slam her doors.

She looked at the strange girl who stared back at her. "You all done?" Kay asked.

"More than done. I'm beat." Shawna slouched into the kitchen and dropped onto one of the chairs. She stretched out her long legs.

"One rule around here is you take off your boots and leave them on the porch when you come in from the barn."

"These are all I've got." Shawna held up one foot. The sole of her tennis shoe was covered with barn muck and straw.

"Well then, take them off. We'll go into town tomorrow and buy you some boots. For now, there're some clean slippers by the back door you can use."

Shawna shrugged, pulled off her sneakers, and tossed them onto the back porch. They landed with a clunk and sent the muck scattering onto the floor.

Kay clenched her teeth. "I put towels in your bathroom, so why don't you go get cleaned up? Dinner will be on the table in an hour. And, Shawna, don't slam the doors when you come and go."

"Another rule?"

Kay nodded.

"Seems like a lot of rules for one place to have." Shawna shuffled through the kitchen and disappeared down the hall, her feet dragging across the wood floor.

"That's gonna be a tough filly to break in." Kenny leaned against the kitchen door.

"How long you been eavesdropping?" Kay asked as she turned up the heat under the potatoes.

He pushed away from the door and went to the sink. "She can do the work. That ain't the problem. It's the charming attitude that's gonna be fun to handle."

"If you got any ideas on what to do, don't sit on your backside and keep it to yourself, okay?"

"I see she's brought your crabby side out," he said, drying his hands and pushing his boots off.

"Sorry." She had no right to snap at him, but she did it now and then. There was nobody else to snap at, so Kenny Fargo got it, took it, and made it better.

She reached into the cupboard for the dishes. *I almost turned him away*, she thought. She shook her head when she remembered Kenny on the lower back step, looking up at her as she stood like a suspicious sentry at her kitchen door.

"I need a place to work and park my trailer," he'd said. "I'll be glad to pay for what I use in the way of water and electricity."

"No. I . . . don't think so." She'd stepped back and pushed the screen door closed.

He took off his hat and held it in front of him, like an old-fashioned suitor in a cowboy western. "I love two things: horses and good whiskey," he said. "And I never mix those pleasures."

She recognized the honesty in his words and in the way he looked at her. She also recognized how much it cost him to beg. So she hired him and later that day, she fought to keep him when Peter told her that Kenny had to go.

"You don't know a thing about the man, Kay. Are you insane?" Peter yelled when she told him what she'd done.

"We could use the help. What harm can it do? He can park his trailer behind the barn, so you won't even have to see it." She could still hear her voice—the way it sounded—a bit scared and yet firm. Every fight they'd had that year, she'd heard her voice always a little fearful, yet becoming firmer with each argument.

"He's got the look of war about him. One of those derelict Vietnam vets with no end of problems." Peter grasped the back of the kitchen chair, his knuckles turning white.

"He stays. We need him."

He'd smiled at her, his lips tight and the message bitter. Then he'd left the kitchen without saying another word.

"Leave the past where it should be. You've got enough to manage in the present," she mumbled to herself.

"You say something?" Kenny called from the back porch.

"Just thinking out loud." She lifted two plates from the cupboard and set them on the table. Then, shaking her head, she took down a third one and pulled up another chair. So her perfectly ordered life had taken a turn, and now she was headed down a road that had more ruts than the one leading to her property. How was she going to manage a sixteen-year-old girl? And this wasn't just any teenaged girl. Shawna may not have come with suitcases, but she sure came with some heavy baggage. This little gal was an iceberg, and Kay felt like the *Titanic*.

Chapter 9

Shawna

"Take a bath, Shawna. Curry the horse, Shawna. Don't slam the doors, Shawna. Do this, Shawna, do that." There are more rules around this place than at the blackjack tables. I close my eyes and lean against the bathroom door.

I do not care.

I do not care.

I can't shake that song out of my head. I saw this Yoga class on TV once, where all the people were trying to turn themselves into pretzels. When they weren't doing that, they were sitting around chanting "*ohm*" over and over—looking like they were zoning out. Well, that doesn't do it for me. *I do not care. I do not care.* Now that makes sense.

I look into the bathroom mirror and sing-song my mantra. Dorky old me shrugs back. Life is getting better, though. Here the mirror isn't cracked, so at least I can see the whole dork.

"Well," I say to the face in the mirror, "I do care about one thing—the way I smell." If I'm not careful, I'll be the one needing a currycomb run down my backside. My hands smell like . . . "Ugh!" *Horse!*

While the tub fills with water, I peel off my socks, jeans, and T-shirt and kick them away. On the shelf, I find bath salts and dump in the contents before I slip into the hot water.

I slide down until my ears fill with the gurgle of underwater sounds. My hair billows like a sea creature around my head, and my arms float up beside me. I feel like my body is separating into parts by weight—the light parts leave the heavier ones on the bottom.

Maybe this is what happens when you die. The soul rises up and strands the heavy part of you back on earth.

I try to imagine how the soul might feel, suddenly set free, without the weight of a head, arms, legs, and all the rest. It reminds me of the time I dreamed I was flying and looked down on all the Las Vegas lights. They were so far away, so beautiful, and I was . . . safe.

"Dinner in ten minutes!" Kay's voice comes through the bathroom door, jolting me awake and onto my feet, sending shock waves through all my body parts.

My first thought is to leap out of the water and make sure I locked the door. Then I remember I'm not in Vegas. I'm not in the apartment. No sweethearts here. Only Kay the Stone and Kenny Fargo, King of Spit.

I stand in the cooled water and shiver.

Don't get soft. Next time check your locks like always.

I grab a towel, dry off, and wrap it around me. My clothes smell bad, even from the corner where I'd kicked them. But then I notice the folded clothes on the back of the toilet. Clean jeans, a long-sleeved plaid shirt, and socks. When I pull them on they're too big, but they smell good and I'm not going to put my horsy clothes back on—no matter what. I roll the jean legs and the shirtsleeves up, pull on the socks, and run my fingers through my wet hair.

I glance in the mirror. "God, I look like I'm ten!" I turn sideways and study my profile. "Maybe eleven." It's the clothes. Who'd ever wear stuff like this?

When I open the bathroom door, food smells wake up my stomach. I haven't had anything since that ham sandwich hours ago and I'm in the mood for chow. I make it down the hall, past where I'll sleep, Kay's office, and the living room, and walk into the kitchen.

Kenny sits at one end of the table, sipping brown liquid from a shot glass.

"Sit here, Shawna." Kay pulls out a chair and then sits at the other end of the table opposite Kenny.

Under each plate there's a mat, and next to the fork and knife, a napkin made out of cloth, not paper. How am I not going to leave grease marks on it?

Kenny's looking spiffy. Clean shirt, hair slicked back, and . . . check out the hands. No horsy smell anywhere.

Kay looks neatened up too. Her shirt is still plaid, but it's not the same one she was cooking in earlier. I'd be able to pick out her closet in a sec. Three hundred plaid shirts, starched, the collars all facing the same direction on the hangers.

A heaped bowl of fluffy white potatoes sits in the center of the table, and steak sliced and soaking in juice is on a platter next to it. There's lettuce and tomatoes tossed into a salad.

I'm reaching for the potatoes when Kay says, "I'll pass them to you."

"Whatever." I help myself to two big plops and set the bowl down.

"Please pass them on to Kenny."

What? Am I playing football? Pass. Pass. Pass. When do I get to like . . . eat?

I pick up my fork. The steak's coming my way. I put down my fork, take the platter and . . . "I know. Pass."

Kay doesn't smile. I don't think that's something she does.

"Can I eat now?"

Kay presses her lips together like she's going to say something starting with M. Then she switches and says, "Salad," handing me the bowl of tossed greens.

I'm a quick learner, so I pass the salad to Kenny; then I sit back and fold my arms.

Kay snaps her napkin and lays it across her lap.

Okay. I get it. I do the same.

She picks up her fork and waggles it in the air. "Now," she says.

Finally.

Kenny starts in about the gray, her temperature, her meds. I'm swallowing, not sure I've chewed much before I do. This is not ketchup soup or Wong's takeout or even Kirby's special deluxe grease.

The potatoes don't taste like any potatoes I've ever eaten before. *Where did they come from? The tomatoes—my gawd—they're red candy. Can I have more?*

Kay is holding the salad out to me. I guess the answer

is yes, I can have more. And now *passing* is not a problem. I've got that down, along with how Kay likes to be the queen at the dinner table. There are rules here, too. Like napkins and passing and waiting until the right time to eat. User Manual Entry #4: Play the Queen's Rules at Dinner.

Chapter 10

Shawna

"You wear plaid. I don't." I stand inside the small dressing room cubicle, my arms crossed and my jaw set.

I'd said no to everything the clerk and Kay had brought in for me to try.

"Then get dressed and come out here and look yourself," Kay says.

"There's nothing in this crappy store that I'd be caught dead in."

Kay waves the clerk out and waits in the doorway. "Fine. Then we'll go someplace else." She yanks the curtain closed. "I'll meet you outside."

"There's nothing in this whole friggin' town that I'd be caught dead in," I say loud enough for anyone in the store to hear. I pull my *Bad Ass Attitude* shirt over my head and jam my feet into my shoes.

On the way out, the two clerks look at me and then away, like they don't want me to see them seeing me— like if our eyes locked, they'd have to sterilize their eyeballs. They whisper behind me, sending little *wis-wis* sounds to follow me outside.

At the door, I turn around. "Hey, Chicas!"

I've got their attention. "Screw you!" I tuck my hair behind my ears and slam the door behind me.

Kay stands, leaning on her truck fender. "Nice, Shawna."

"I'm sick of this shopping crap."

Kay arches her neck like her horses do whenever they go ornery. Right now, her neck tells me I'm in for a fight—one I'd lose. "Fine. You can wear my jeans and one of my plaid shirts to school."

I shift my weight to one foot and stick out my left hip. "All right." I'm giving in, but I want her to know it's only this time. "But you gotta take me someplace that's got clothes, not cowgirl getups."

Her look could shrivel a Vegas pit boss I swear.

"Get in." Kay climbs into her battered truck. "We are going to Sacramento." She starts the engine. "Buckle up. And from now on, drop the tacky language."

This ride is like the others: silent, except for the whir of traffic outside and her truck, of course. It rattles so much I expect parts to shake free and hurtle into the cars behind us. She never turns on the radio, and I'm sure from the way she looks she won't let me turn it on either, so I hum to myself. This used to drive my mom up the wall, so I hope it will get to Kay too. That's exactly what I want to do for the next forty minutes—push all her buttons. Rile her up. See her turn red-in-the-face angry. I'll show her who's callin' the shots about work, about clothes, about my life.

When she pulls into a parking lot and gets out I follow, dragging my shoes over the steamy asphalt. Push a button here. Push a button there. Push a . . . she disappears inside a store without turning around to look at me.

She's pissed.

I enter the store and find her waiting next to the drinking fountain just inside.

"Here's three hundred dollars." She holds out three single bills. "I'll meet you here when you're done."

I work on looking casual when I take the money. I don't say anything. But when I do a one-eighty and scuff my way to the racks, I roll my eyes at the three hundred bucks Kay just plunked in my hand. *That's the electric bill, the water bill, a few movie tickets, and some burgers with curly fries. Maybe even a rehabbed air conditioner, one that actually works all the time. Living with Kay might be cushier than I thought.*

I look around the store. This place holds more promise. Other girls with some style savvy are alongside me, pawing through the clothes. I take my time, and once in a while glance toward the drinking fountain. There she is: Kay Stone, looking like she's the store greeter, with nothing better to do than stand where she is.

When I've loaded my left arm with possible buys, the clerk counts out my allotted seven items and unlocks a dressing room.

"I'll check back," she says and leaves me inside with a three-way mirror under fluorescent lights that, with my dark eyes and black hair, turns my skin pasty.

Mom used to hate dressing rooms like this, and when it came her turn to try on something, she'd boot me out the door. "You bring me stuff when I need it, okay?" she'd say.

"What's the deal? You watched me with my butt hanging out."

"Shut up, Shawna." And in a few minutes she'd stick her hand out, dangle the jeans or the backless top and send me to find another size. Another color. Another style. This would go on a loooong time.

"Well," I asked her once, when she unlocked the door and stepped out after an hour-long dressing-room session. "What are you getting?"

On her index finger she twirled a halter-top.

"That's the one I wanted," I said. "You told me it was too . . . skimpy or some kind of crap like that."

"Who's paying for this, you or me?" She shoved her face close.

I could have said something. Something like, "Who does the kid part of your act?" But I didn't. The halter-top wasn't worth it. I could have said she was a little old to wear clothes from the Junior section. But I didn't. Nothing was worth the hell I'd get for saying that.

Now, without Mom, I take my time under the fluorescents. I pull on pants and a top, turn to check my backside. *Not bad. But maybe no more curly fries for a while.*

I'm into and out of the next outfit before I finish zipping up.

That's totally not happening.

And before I know it, I've tried on everything. In little more than an hour, I've found my Sweet River High wardrobe. I pay the bill and hold out the change to Kay.

"Keep it. But give me the receipt in case you have to bring something back." She folds the receipt and puts it into her pocket. "Come on. We've got work to do."

It's after two when we finally get back to the ranch.

"Put your things away, then come out and do your chores." Kay walks to the barn.

I shrug after she turns her back. I want it clear that I don't care one bit about her, her chores, or even the clothes. Well, maybe the clothes. A little. It's kind of neat to take each piece out and see it in my private space. Sort of like bringing home new friends and getting to know them better.

Chapter 11

Kay

Kay found Kenny leaning against the side of the barn, staring across at Floyd's.

"Looks like you survived the shopping trip!" He gave her his lopsided grin.

"Yes. I would have preferred a long morning in hell." Kay sighed and looked over at the shabby barn on the next ranch. "If I drank in the afternoon, I'd go next door to Floyd's and have a double with him right now."

"You raised one before. You can do it again," he said.

"No. This is different. She's as skittish as a horse new to the saddle. Nicholas never had an edge to him like Shawna has." She closed her eyes and tried to picture the lanky boy with the wide-set eyes that made her feel alive whenever he turned them on her. It was hard now to recall him any other way, except as the young boy who sat between her and Peter in the movies, or galloped ahead of her like he'd been born in that saddle. She couldn't remember him as the man who chose to marry the girl of her nightmares, the man who joined the service, the man who left and never returned.

"She's really got to you," Kenny said.

Kay frowned, drawing her dark brows together. "Truth is she worries me—a lot."

Kenny nodded. "Something's under her saddle, and you'd best find out what before too long."

"Are you trying to scare me more than I am already?"

"Nope. Just giving my opinion. I charge for advice," he said, pushing away from the barn and heading toward Floyd's.

"Now what are you up to?" she called after him.

"Same as always. Those horses of Floyd's are out of water again. They may as well have water. They don't have much else."

"What about the gray? Any change?"

He shook his head. "She's better, but I'm keeping in touch with the vet. Might give her a turn around the place to stretch her legs."

Kenny climbed over the top rail and walked across Floyd's property. He walked slower these days, but with the same side-to-side cowboy sway. Once she'd asked him how a cowboy wound up a Vietnam medic.

"Every war needs a good cowboy, don't you know that?" He'd looked off into the distance before answering. " 'Sides, I needed a place to hide out. Nobody was gonna go after me in one of them soggy rice paddies."

She'd wanted in the worst way to say, "Hide out?" But she'd only looked at him with the question in her eyes.

"I never said I was a saint, did I?" he asked.

She smiled again as she had that day. *St. Kenny. That*

has a nice sound to it, she thought as she watched Kenny fill Floyd's watering trough. The horses clustered around, dipping their heads low and drinking under the hot sun.

If I had the money, she thought, *I'd buy those horses and put them out to pasture. Someday I'll do that. Someday I'll buy Floyd out. He needs to live somewhere else, where he doesn't have that burned-down house to look at everyday, a place where the memories aren't so horrible.*

She clenched her jaw. The memories of that night were horrible to her as well, even after all these years. She still felt the lick of flames on her face, heard Floyd's screams, saw herself in slow-motion running behind Peter and Nicholas, feeding the water hose to its full length. She wished she could erase those pictures forever. She hated it when they flashed through her head and made her chest tight with regret. Now there was Shawna. More regret, another reason to be tense. She sighed. She had to do something to get her mind off the past and her troubling granddaughter for a while.

She looked into the barn. Kenny was right; exercise might do the gray some good. Kay saddled the mare and set her down the trail at a slow walk. She followed her property line to the creek, and then cut across the water and up the other side, where the hill crested onto an open meadow of August-brown grass. The gray seemed to perk up, so she nudged her sides with her heels and the horse shot forward, eager to stretch her legs. Kay felt that surge of power under her, and thoughts of the past and Shawna vanished.

She could still sit a horse, even at sixty. Well, okay,

sixty-four. Her one lie, and even Kenny didn't know it was a lie. She didn't tell it to be coy; she told it to give herself a future, because if she hung around long enough, the good had to start outweighing all the bad.

She smiled and gently drew up on the reins. "Okay, old girl, let's take it slow for awhile before we pull something." *Was she talking to the horse or herself? Maybe both.*

The gray seemed suddenly sluggish, so Kay slid from the saddle and walked her slowly up the hill.

She and Peter and Nicholas had come this way so many times that she didn't think about where she was going. The trail wound around an open meadow and back to the creek in an easy loop that took about an hour. She'd be back in time to help finish the chores and make dinner, and do everything she did every night.

But now Shawna was back in her mind. What Kay understood about teenage girls was close to nothing. They were aliens who spoke a different language, dressed with more body parts showing than if they were in their bedrooms, and pierced themselves in places that made her cringe. At least Shawna wasn't punched full of holes, not ones she could see, anyway. Kay made a mental note to ask about that later. And what about tattoos?

She'd never imagined doing anything close to what the girls did nowadays, but she'd grown up in the good old days, the fifties. The year she turned fifteen, Elvis shocked the world with his swivel hips that sent the censors into cardiac arrest. But there was that Spring Break her last high school year. Kay fit her boot into the stirrup and slung her leg across the gray. She leaned back in the saddle and gave the gray her head.

"Take your time," she said, and stroked the firm neck.

The picture of that April day in 1957 always came clear and strong, refusing to fade. Yet it wasn't an important day at all, compared to others that followed. Her mother had stood looking pinched as a drawstring bag, and her grandmother gazed across the table like she'd been stunned by a blow to the head. They were in Mom's kitchen, and she'd just come back from Nancy Kendal's slumber party. *Strange*, she thought, stroking the gray's neck, *I can smell that spice cake sitting on the table, as if Gram had just baked it*. She could even hear her mother's voice.

"What possessed you?" her mother shouted, but she didn't wait for an explanation. Instead, she wrung her hands like she was rehearsing Lady Macbeth and asked, "What were you thinking?"

"Everybody's doing it, Mom. It's only a little bleach, for gosh sakes."

"A little? Your hair is orange!"

It was true. Nancy's had turned a creamy yellow, but then she'd started with light brown hair. Kay had to admit she was disappointed with the orange, but frankly she'd been afraid to add more bleach. Her hair might fall out, and then what would she do? "It'll grow out."

"And what a fine mess that's going to be. A nice black line down the center of your head. You'll be able to join the circus." Her mother picked up her purse. "Well, you're not going out like that, so I guess we'll have to dye it back."

"Where are you going?" Kay yelled.

"To the drug store," her mother yelled back. "And you be here, young lady, when I get home."

The gray mare reached the creek and stopped midway across for a drink.

How can I compare bleached hair with what the kids do today, she asked herself, sitting taller in the saddle. *I can't.*

She sighed, wishing she could explain to her mom how fashionable orange hair had now become. She'd just been a few decades ahead of her time.

Kay tried to remember the rest of that day, but it had slipped away to some part of her brain that couldn't or wouldn't recall it. *How long ago had that happened, anyway?* she wondered. *Fifty years? More than half a life.*

It was time to get back to this other half of her life. The half not lived yet with all of its uncertainty, especially about Shawna.

"Oh, Kay, what have you gotten yourself into?" she asked aloud.

The gray snorted.

"I know. We have to try. Right, girl?" Kay leaned over the gray and laid her cheek against the warm gray neck.

Chapter 12

Shawna

I'm forking clean straw into the stalls when Kay walks in, leading the gray horse, both of them in a sweat. The gray doesn't walk like the other horses. She struts with her neck curved and her tail in a high arch. When I first saw her in the barn with the other horses, I told Kenny how I thought she moved. He told me she was a princess, and when I laughed he drew up very serious, saying, "An Arabian princess." Then he spit. "And don't forget it."

Kay stops in front of me. "Walk her around the barn a few times; then wipe her down," she says, and turns the gray over to me.

Walking a horse is way easier than pitching hay. I walk her real slowly to give her a chance to cool down, and to give myself a chance to rest before going back to finish up in the barn. I've been working for four days, doing the same thing over again and again.

"This is wack!" I shout to the sky, like somebody might actually care.

The gray noses me from behind, and I stumble.

"Dumb horse!" But then who's the dumb one here? I'm doing all the work, and she's about to get a rub down from yours truly.

When I tie her off, she leans into me and I feel her sweat against my arm. I should be weirded out but I'm not. Horse sweat isn't what it was four days ago.

I slip the gray's saddle and blanket off, then wipe her down like Kenny's shown me. She shakes her long neck and nuzzles her head against me.

"Like that, huh?" I ask.

She nuzzles harder like she understands me. She pushes her nose against my hair and snuffles so my scalp tingles.

Too bad she's just a horse.

"Hey now," I say, as she dips her head. If she were a person, she could get a massage whenever she wanted one. I know some massage parlors that would go wild over her.

She snorts and shakes her head.

"Horsing around, are you?" *Shawna, you are ready for stand up on the Vegas Strip.*

I finish with the gray and put her in her stall.

"Bye, beautiful," I whisper; then I slap my face to bring myself around. *Get a grip, Shawna. This is a temporary gig. No bonding with the locals, okay?*

By six my arms give out like always, but that happens conveniently at the same time as my jobs are done, so I consider it my lucky day. I'm dragging myself back to the house when I hear a loud crack, like a gunshot. I drop to my knees behind a barrel Kay's planted with geraniums. When I look around the side, I don't see anyone bearing down on me with a six-shooter. So I get up slowly and look across at the shack on the other side of Kay's fence, where the sound came from.

A man is staggering out of the barn and toward the fence. The three sick-looking horses are huddled together at the fence closest to Kay's property. I can't see their eyes, but I know they're wide because their ears are laid back and they're being what Kenny calls *skittery*. I never know if he's giving me real words, but I use them anyway.

The man holds a coil of rope in his fist. He stops before he reaches the fence, lays the coil out in front of him, then raises his hand and yanks on the rope until it cracks overhead. It's a whip, not a rope. And, most important, there's not a gun in sight. The horses crush into each other, and the black horse slams against Kay's fence so hard that the posts wobble.

I walk closer. Either the man doesn't see me or he's blind. I'm at the fence, and, if I want, I can touch the black horse that's pressed hard against the rail. It tosses its head and shies away from me. It's actually stuck between a rock and a hard place. That old man with the whip is coming up from one side, and I, a stranger, am standing on the other.

The horse reminds me of a kid I saw once, who got caught between a gang and the cops. Their eyes look the same and, like the horse, the kid pressed himself against the building as if by pressing hard enough he could get on the other side of the bricks and escape. I never knew how that standoff ended because the cops dragged me down the street to ask me questions.

"Hey!" I yell across the horses' backs. The black

horse tries to rear, but the other two have him pinned. He can't do more than raise his head and dig into the dirt with his front hooves.

The old jerk sees me all right. He isn't blind, but he's totally smashed. He stops and nearly loses his balance. The whip trails from his hand like a tail he's lopped off of some poor animal.

"Git outta here!" he slurs.

"You git outta here, you old jerk! And leave these horses alone."

A sick grin spreads across his face. I've seen those kinds of faces late at night outside the casinos—mean drunks on their way to do something bad to anybody who gets in their way. Weaving on his feet, he coils the whip and starts toward me. The horses bolt around his backside and disappear behind the barn. I hold my ground as he comes closer. I've seen enough drunks to know that all I have to do with this one is give him a shove and he'll fall flat on his butt.

Now here's something I never thought I'd hear myself say: "How about I call the cops, old man? You like the idea of going to the slammer?" I must sound like I know what I'm talking about, because he draws up short and stands unsteady like he's in a shallow boat.

Even from across the fence, the smell of gin and stale tobacco make me want to puke. When he opens his mouth I take a step away, but his stench follows.

"Stay off a . . . my prop . . . property."

"She's not on yer property, Floyd." Kenny Fargo's voice is loud at my back.

I scream and spin around. "Man, you about gave me a heart attack!"

Kenny ignores me and walks straight at Floyd. "Yer drunk. Go to bed or I'll call the cops myself." Then Kenny turns to me. "You ought not take on Floyd when he's drunk and has his whip. Now, go on inside. I've got some things to do. Tell Kay I'll be late for dinner." Kenny flings his leg over the top rail of the fence and jumps down onto Drunk Floyd's side.

He walks alongside Floyd, his hand on his back until they reach the shack. Then Floyd staggers up the steps, dragging the whip like a dead snake, and disappears inside. I stay put, ignoring Kenny's orders about going in the house. Kenny walks to the water trough and, one by one, the three horses come out from hiding. They nuzzle Kenny's back, then dip into the trough for a drink. Kenny goes into the barn and the horses follow him.

Country people are way weirder than city ones. I start toward the house. Kay puts dinner on the table at the same time, so I figure I have ten minutes to clean up. It feels weird to know what's going to happen every day and when it's going to happen.

At dinner, there's no mention about Drunk Floyd or my little meeting with the neighbor, but the clothes subject rears up when Kenny Fargo asks what we did all day.

"She's going to give us a fashion show a little later. Right?" Kay levels her eyes at me.

"Why?"

"Because Kenny and I want to see what you chose."

"I got good stuff."

68

"I know you did, but we still need to see the things you bought."

"Hell."

"I thought you understood about the language, Shawna."

"Sh . . ."

"I wouldn't push it," Kay interrupts. "I mean it." She points her finger at my face.

I shove my plate forward and rock my chair backward on two legs. What is with her, anyway? I don't think my language is bad. I'd cleaned up all the F-words so I didn't sound like Mom, and so my teachers wouldn't stick me in the hall anymore. Compared to the real world, I sound as clean as an elf in Santa's workshop.

"I'll get the dishes tonight," Kenny says, standing up from the table and carrying his plate to the kitchen sink. "You two duke it out without me."

"There's nothing to fight over. I'll give you your dumb fashion show." I remember Mom's advice. Pick your fights. Besides, I'm way too tired to go toe to toe with Kay tonight.

I put on one outfit after the other, and stomp back and forth between my room and the kitchen. They inspect me like they do their horses, but they don't say anything. *Well, duh! Nothing new about that.*

"This is the last one." I've saved my Diesels and the halter top to the end.

"Too tight across the backside and too skimpy on the top. Those go back," Kay says.

I open my mouth but I don't get a chance to say what I want.

"The rest are good choices, Shawna." She gets up from her chair. I almost expect her to stamp *approved* on my forehead, but she doesn't even glance at me as she walks past.

Kenny Fargo smiles. "I thought the first one was the best, the black and red. Good colors on you." He turns back to the sink and sprinkles cleanser over the scarred surface.

I liked the Diesels. I wanted the Diesels. Now I want them even more, since they have to go back. I stomp into my room and slam the door.

Who does she think she is anyway, the fashion police? I'm outta here. I've given this dump four days of my time and that's all the patience I've got.

I grab a shopping bag and stuff the Diesels inside. *She can keep the rest. Screw her.* I'm down the hall and past her office before she can say anything. Out the door, I give it a good bang. I pound down the front steps and go around Buster, who's stretched out at the bottom. He jumps up and follows me. "Go away, flea bag." He sits on the road and whines, just like I've hurt his feelings.

In the dark it's hard to miss all the ruts in this road, so it's very slow going. I'm picking my way like I'm on the edge of the Grand Canyon. Finally, when I get to the paved road, my brain decides to wake up. *This is a big mistake, Shawna. It's totally black out here.*

No cars. Nobody to hitch a ride from. I'm stranded. It's miles in any direction. *Where's a cab when you need one?*

I've got no choice. I turn back down the road, to the

house where Buster thumps his tail and jumps, doing his midair spin.

"Stupid dog." I scratch the back of his neck and he settles down.

Stupid Shawna is more like it.

I bang my way back into the house, stomp down the hall, ignore Kay who is still sitting behind her desk, and she gives me a look over the top of her glasses. I slam the door when I get to the end of the hall.

Just one more little button push for the day.

Chapter 13

Shawna

When September shows up, Sweet River turns as hot as asphalt on a Vegas parking lot. I've survived three weeks of Kay's summer camp for stray grandkids, made it through the high school entry exam, and endured long nights with the windows cranked wide and the fan whirring above my bed while I read what the long-gone Mark Twain had to say on just about every topic in the world.

I caught some kind of bug—probably from that fan whipping air down on my head all night—so I've already missed the first week of school. But tomorrow Kay and I have an appointment with the school principal. I considered begging off and playing like I'm still sick, but Kay has a nose for liars that would land her a security job at the Casino Royale.

I close the book on Mr. Twain's advice and turn out the light. Round as one of those old Vegas dollars, the moon hangs above the trees. It spreads silver across the floor and the end of the bed. If I melted all the money

Mom dropped in the casinos, it might look just like this. The fan drones overhead; it sounds like a tired helicopter. *Frap. Frap. Frap.* I bury my head under the pillow.

"Damn." I reach up and turn the fan off. I'd rather roast than hear it droning overhead.

A coyote howl travels from a corner of the ranch, across the pasture, past the barn, and through my window. It's a lonely sound that catches me in the stomach. My memories are stored right there, behind my belly button, just under the skin, instead of in my brain, like where normal people have them.

Sometimes they gather up and push hard, like they want out. I'd pierce my belly button in a sec just to shake the total dork image, but what happens if those memories ooze out?

Stop it. Don't think so much. That always gets you in trouble.

I bury my head under my pillow. That used to work when I was a kid and alone, waiting for Mom to come home. Waiting. That was hard sometimes, and scary.

Don't be a wimp. Lock the door and don't open it. I'll be back by three. She always sounded impatient, like I was being stupid.

The high and lonely howl comes again, only from another direction and closer. Another coyote. I picture two lonely creatures out there, circling, looking.

Oh, no. I'm getting the shakes, and . . . I don't believe it. Monster's here. So he did come with me to Sweet River. The sirens in Vegas used to wake him up. Now it's coyotes howling in the night. City. Country. He's everywhere.

73

It's him, all right. Dark and shadowy.

I open the nightstand drawer and for a moment hold the plastic bottle filled with Mom's sleeping pills. Then I pull out the slim toilet paper bundle, unroll the razor blade, and hold it out to him in my palm.

"See?" I whisper to him. "It's right here."

He creeps out and sits hunched at the foot of the bed.

I take the blade between my thumb and first finger—no easy trick when the shakes come over me.

I already know how it's going to feel. How it's going to open old scars from other times—those crooked lines that turn to scabs and pucker the skin under my ankle bone.

But I know once the blade slides inside me, I don't hurt, I don't think, I don't shake anymore. For one delicious moment, I'm not afraid of Monster or anybody else.

I have a half inch red streak and a tiny trickle of blood that I blot with the toilet paper. Monster's slipping away, over the edge of the bed. He'll be gone in another second. My hands are steady now, so it's easy to wrap the blade and tuck it into the drawer. By the time I turn back he's gone, and the coyotes now are silent. Without the *frap, frap* of the fan, there isn't any sound.

Now I can finally sleep. The memories will be good. They will be about sweet ice cream on a spoon, and me laughing.

The knock at the door sends my heart to my toes. I'm beginning to think about the downside of doors.

"Shawna, are you awake?"

It's Kay.

Chapter 14

Kay

Kay worked in her office almost every night after dinner. And now that the house was filled with Shawna, her smells, her sounds, but mostly her anger, Kay clung to the certainty of numbers to help focus on something other than Shawna's explosive, unpredictable nature.

Tonight the numbers weren't as certain as she'd like. *This darned checkbook won't balance*, she thought. She was adding the figures a second time when Shawna shuffled down the hall past the office. "Goodnight," Kay called.

"Right." Shawna didn't stop on the way to her room.

Kay waited for the slam of the door.

Bam!

She stood partway up; then shook her head. No. She wouldn't rise to the bait. What could she do anyway, spank the girl? For a moment she closed her eyes, before returning to the numbers that wouldn't add up.

She finally pushed her chair away from her desk and, rubbing her eyes, laid her glasses on the pile of invoices.

She'd finish them tomorrow, after she dropped Shawna at school.

Why was she nervous about Shawna's first day at Sweet River High? Shawna certainly didn't seem to be. Kay stretched her back. Maybe that's what worried her. The girl didn't care about anything. Would Shawna continue her shrugging indifference at school? What would the school do in return?

I can't worry about what might happen, she thought. *And I can't change what's already come around the corner of the barn*. She turned off the lights and walked into the hall.

She made her way to Shawna's door. She'd just check to see if she was feeling better. Maybe she should tell her to go back to town and get the Diesels. Those tight-fitting jeans seemed to be the crux of Shawna's pout for the last two weeks. No. Her granddaughter would not look like a hooker. Kay raised her hand to knock, but stopped when she heard Shawna's voice.

"See? It's right here."

Kay waited, her ear turned to the door. Who could she be talking to? She didn't have a cell phone. There was no phone in her bedroom. She listened again, but Shawna didn't say anything else. Kay knocked. "You awake?"

Small sounds like whispers came from inside, but Shawna didn't answer her.

"Shawna. Are you all right?"

"Yeah." Shawna said.

A drawer slid open or closed, and the bed shifted, like Shawna was climbing in or out. But no footsteps came toward the door.

"May I come in?" Kay asked.

"It's your house."

Kay saw the shrug even from behind the door. With a sigh, she turned the knob and pushed the door open. "I just wondered how you were feeling." She glanced around the room. The window stood open, the fan was still. Shawna lay under the sheet and a small dark stain, still wet, spread across the white cotton. "Did you scratch yourself?" Kay asked.

"Oh, yeah." Shawna tucked her leg under the blanket. "Mosquito bite, but I'm okay. It's stopped bleeding."

"I thought I heard you say something."

"Thinking out loud, I guess." Shawna sat up. "Is there a rule against that?"

"No." Kay turned to leave. "Do you want one?"

Shawna laughed. "Not!"

Kay pulled the door shut behind her and leaned against it. She smiled. Had they just joked with each other?

Chapter 15

Kay

The next day Kay drove Shawna to school, and they made their way to the office. The principal's door stood open, so Kay knocked on the doorjamb to get his attention. "Robby?"

Shawna glanced at Kay, looking puzzled.

"Kay." A pudgy man in a brown tweed jacket stood to greet them. "Good to meet you, Shawna." He nodded. "Please have a seat."

He shuffled through a stack of folders with his stubby fingers and pulled one out. "These scores are very interesting," he said without looking at either of them sitting on the other side of the desk. "Very interesting."

Shawna's eyes were focused on her feet, but at the mention of test scores, she looked first at the principal and then at Kay, then drew herself up tight as a feral cat cornered in the barn.

"Shawna's education has been irregular." Kay said. She shifted in her chair. She never explained anything when she was dealing with her own business, so she felt uncomfortable hearing her voice spill out excuses, especially in front of Robby Green, who already knew more about her than she wanted. Still, she couldn't stop. "Her mother . . ." Kay's throat felt suddenly dry and she swallowed before finishing. ". . . moved a great deal."

No matter how many years had passed, whenever she remembered that dark-haired girl with the darting eyes and the nervous mouth, her whole body reacted like she was coming down with something.

"That makes these results even more fascinating." He put the papers on the desk and leaned back in his chair. It squeaked under his bulk. "They are off the charts."

"I can arrange for a tutor," Kay said.

The principal sat up and put his elbows on his desk. "I'm afraid you don't understand. Shawna scored extremely high on her tests. Her verbal, math, and reading scores are impressive. Her essay was," he glanced at Shawna, "very adult and shows a sophisticated level of writing ability. She doesn't need a tutor. In fact, she could be a tutor around here."

Kay looked at Shawna, whose face she knew and whose sticky moods and bad language she was trying to manage. Now she studied that face, mining for the brilliance this school's tests had revealed. "I'm surprised, of course, but very pleased. What do we do about someone with 'off-the-chart' test scores?"

"She's a candidate for the advanced placement program. We have an AP Coordinator here, so I'll arrange a meeting. We'll see that she's challenged. And we should probably get her started as soon as possible." He looked at Shawna, who was biting her thumbnail to the quick. "Are you ready for the first day in your new high school?"

Chapter 16

Shawna

I don't say a word while Robby and Granny discuss me. When he asks me if I'm ready to go to school, I want to shout, "Dumb question." This is like the tenth school I've been to in the last three years, and they're all the same to me: The prissy blonds look out from eyeballs they've chilled in the fridge before class, and they won't talk to each other until you pass them in the hall; then they lay you out. The jocks just released from a field or a court want to paw you, and then put you down when you don't roll over panting. The gangs are really terrific minefields, and then there're the nerds. I feel like asking, "You got some level of hell I can go to? I'll take one of those, please."

Instead, I zip it and I follow Mr. Rolly-Poly Robby down the corridor, wondering how Kay knows him so well, and if that's going to work for or against me in this school. When I step into the AP English class, the teacher sticks a piece of paper into one hand and a book into the other and points to a seat. I'm just in time to write a thirty-minute essay.

I'm glad I'm not rolling dice today, with the kind of luck I'm having. A principal on a first-name basis with Granny *and* a timed essay. I suck in my cheeks and bite down.

I get a back seat, which is good and not so good. The good part is I can sit with my back to the wall and nobody behind me. The not-so-good part is I have to walk down the whole row with all those eyes staring up into my face. Nerd, nerd, two sets of icy blue eyes, one jock, and—uh oh, one category I forgot—a troll.

More luck. I get to sit in the back with a troll for company. Oh well, it could be worse. But then, when I sit down, I get a closer look at the girl's ferret-stare and catch a whiff of that loamy smell. Trolls don't know about soap.

I glance up at the teacher, Mrs. Heady. She's been around chalk dust a long time. She's also embraced Sweet River's dress code. I never knew they made whole dresses out of plaid. Pencils sprout from the back of her head like spores seeking light, and every once in a while she reaches back, plucks one out, scribbles a note, then tucks the pointed end back into her coiled braid. She makes it hard for me to concentrate on the essay, but I finally manage to shut her out and read the question.

"It is easier to tell the truth than to tell a lie. Do you agree or disagree with this topic statement? Support your position with one or two specific examples from personal experience, events past or present, or from books you have read. (Three paragraphs minimum. 30 minutes.)"

Pathetic. Who thinks up these essay questions anyway?

I pull out my Casino Royale ballpoint and write Shawna across the top of the paper. This is an interesting dilemma—di . . . lem . . .ma. I love that word. It means something terrible, but it rolls off the tip of my tongue and sounds delicious. Do I put down the truth, or do I give her what she'd like to read?

I look at the clock.

I better decide or I'm not going to get anything down.

I disagree with the proposition that it is easier to tell the truth than it is to tell a lie. There are times when a lie works a lot better than the truth. I come from Las Vegas, a town where lying is an art form, so I have a lot of examples to support my position. In fact, I have so many that three hundred paragraphs wouldn't be enough space to write them out.

Let's take a bar girl for example. She wouldn't make any tips if she told the drunk how flat-out ugly he was. Instead, by saying he's a handsome so and so, giving him a small pat on his butt and a smile that tells him he's the only guy she's looking at, the girl takes home enough dough to cover her rent and her child care for the month.

Sometimes it's better to lie than to hurt somebody with the truth. If a dorky guy asks a girl out and she would rather drink rat poison than be seen in public with him, I think she should tell him she's got a date for that night. That way he saves face and she's off the hook. Imagine a friend who is overweight asking for an "honest" opinion about how she looks wearing her new, very tight pants. Talk about a minefield! If she looks fat and you tell her so, you can kiss that friendship good-bye. There are tons of times like these when people lie, and lying makes life better for the one being lied to and for the person telling the lie, too.

Okay, I have two paragraphs of examples—that's more than enough. But, no, English teachers have this essay-trinity-thing they want. So, what can I use for the third?

I could write about me. I close my eyes and think about the next paragraph. Something like,

If I told the truth about what my mom does for a living, I'd be in Juvie and she'd be in jail. My mom's a gambler and sometimes a pickpocket when she's down on her luck, so, as anyone can see, if I'd told the truth to the police when they came to visit a few months ago, I wouldn't be sitting here now, trying to defend my preference for lying.

No. I don't want to write that. Let's keep this essay impersonal.

Think about the politicians and how none of them would be elected if they told the truth. "I'm going to raise taxes the first chance I get." "I'm declaring war as soon as I can make up an excuse." Would these truthful candidates win? I don't think so.

I reread the four paragraphs.

Not really good. I need a way more interesting question to write about if I'm going to bend my brain and be brilliant on paper. I lean back and twirl my pen. If I shake it up, maybe some punchy idea will flow out in the ink. A quote, maybe. That's one thing I always surprise people with. They can tell me something, and it's in and out of my head in a snap, but let me read it somewhere, and it sticks there like glue.

So what quotes do I know about lying?

Even Mark Twain wrote in one of his letters to a friend, "I would rather tell seven lies than make one explanation." Well, I agree with Mr. Twain. I know people would rather hear something they like than something they don't. I know that sometimes the truth causes more damage than it does good, and sometimes it's more trouble to explain than to lie.

Ta da! The summary conclusion, and it's a wrap. I look up at the clock. I still have ten minutes before Mrs. Heady collects the papers, so I open the textbook she handed me on my way in and start the reading assignment written on the board. It doesn't take long to lose myself in the story for tomorrow's discussion, so I don't see Mrs. Heady until she's hovering over me.

"And what are you doing?" she asks, leaning over and whispering in my ear.

I want to say something like, "Eating cookie dough. What do you think?" "Reading," I say, telling the truth.

"You've finished your essay?"

I nod and hand her my paper. She's on her way to the front of the room when she stops with her back to me. If she'd been a car, she would have skidded and spun out. She brings my paper closer to her face, cranks her head side to side like she's trying to rid her neck of a nasty crick, and then turns to look at me over her shoulder.

I shrug and lower my eyes to the Aesop Fable about a boy and a wolf.

Chapter 17

Shawna

I survive my first week in Sweet River High and wake up to Sunday quiet. On Sundays the ranch is a whole different world. Instead of whistling his horses to him, Kenny Fargo sits on the front porch with his feet propped on the rail, reading the paper. Kay doesn't stomp down the back steps toward the barn, either. She spends the day in her office. Even Buster isn't up and doing his weekday job. There's no nipping at the sheep to keep them out of the garden; instead he stretches out in a sunny patch like funky yard art.

Kay comes out of the kitchen with a mug of coffee in her hand, and passes me as I'm looking out the window at rural America, wondering why I ever got on that bus leaving Vegas.

"There's toast and cereal on the table, Shawna. I've got paperwork to do," she says before closing her office door behind her.

Sunday is about as exciting as having a conversation with one of Kay's sheep. I almost miss not being dragged out to the barn.

I eat breakfast, read the back of the cereal box, and time how long I can hold my breath. I know all about nightmares, but Sunday is a double nightmare. I push myself away from the table, grab an apple, and cut it into chunks. Time to do something. Anything!

When I walk past the barn, two Sunday boys are working. One is cleaning stalls and another is in the tack room, working on a saddle. The one using my favorite rake gets my attention. I love how his jeans hug his butt. He turns and catches me staring.

"Hi." He smiles and waves at me.

I don't want any cozy communication with him, so I shrug and look away.

When he goes back to raking, I notice he digs the rake in a little deeper. And I'm thinking he needles pretty easy, and that should be fun when I'm bored around this place. But then there are those jeans. I wander over to the fence to scope out Drunk Floyd's place. The old man isn't outside. I wait to see if he might pop out of his barn or come out from behind one of those big oaks on the other side of his shack.

When I'm pretty sure Drunk Floyd is sleeping it off somewhere, I climb the fence and work my way around the block foundation where it's clear this place went up in flames. Inside the knee-high walls, charcoal chunks lie scattered among the weeds, sprouting around the junk—an oven door, a sink, a bucket. A limp vine has a strangle hold on some rusty mattress springs, and gophers are mining the ground from side to side.

I go slow and quiet over to the black horse. He keeps

his head down, but he eyes me with every step I take toward him. I get within three feet before he flattens his ears and backs off. I take the chunks of apple out of the napkin and hold them in my palm. He shakes his head and plows the ground with his front hoof, but he doesn't come closer. I sit down, keeping my hand out. Still, he doesn't move toward me. I know he wants this apple the way he dips his head, but he keeps five feet of space between us, watching.

"I'm a little tired of this, black horse. Either you come over here or I eat this damned apple."

He swishes his tail and eyes me.

"Okay, I'm lying down. The apple's yours, but you gotta make the move." I stretch out and put the apple on my stomach.

The sun is hot and the weeds prickle my back and my legs. I wonder what creepy Tuan is up to right now? And Mom. What's she doing? I think about her dark hair and the way it used to shine after she washed it and let it dry in the hot desert sun. When I squint my eyes real hard, I can see her face—the plummy red she painted on her lips before she went out, her eyes and the thick matted lashes she coated until they turned into dark fringe. The way . . . *Stop!*

Monster is combing through the weeds and the shakes are right behind him, so I push the heels of my hands into my eyes. Remember something else, Shawna. *Remember Mom's face when it turned ugly on you. Yeah!*

"You want to be the star? Is that it, Shawna?"

Remember that? Mom pacing back and forth, arms crossed, jutting her chin out and staring me down.

"Well, you can't be. You hear? Me. I'm the star in this family."

She hammered me, and all I did was put on her red dress. The veins in her neck stuck out like they might snap, and her lips drew back so I could see her gums.

"All I wanted was to—"

"Shut up." She pulled back her hand and I caught it on its way to my face. I never used to duck. I never used to stop her. That day things changed between us. She stepped away and put her hands on both hips. "Don't sass me." She grabbed the red dress out of my hand and threw it on the bed. "And stay the hell out of my things."

Yes, Shawna, remember when your mother turned on you. The shakes are gone.

I feel something nudge my belly. I almost jump to my feet, but I catch myself and keep very still. I squint up at the great dark horse hovering over me, drawing the apple chunks between his lips. His mouth brushes against my shirt. The heat of his breath filters through to my skin.

"Yes," I whisper.

No. My heart pumps in my throat.

Get away.

Run.

I clench my fists as he takes more of the apple. It's scary.

Why? This isn't some . . . guy.

Then why?

It's scary because . . . I swallow . . . *I like it.*

My throat feels as if it's stuffed with cotton balls as the horse's warm puffs of breath flow across my belly.

This is not the way to stay safe.
Now who are you talking to?
I'm talking to you, girlfriend. Listen up, Shawna!

He finishes the apple and shies away. I watch him disappear inside the barn.

I sit up, but I can't even stand. My bones are Jell-O. Man, this is too strange. My eyes burn, and that's not natural for me. A little kid, maybe. Not Shawna.

"Crap!" Saying that out loud helps bring me back to normal. I push myself to my feet and swipe my arm across my eyes.

Drunk Floyd must have come to just about the time I swing my leg over the fence and drop back to the other side. He staggers out his door and down his back steps toward his car. He yanks open the door and falls in behind the wheel. The old stick shift groans when he shoves it into reverse, and the car rolls backwards, sort of like it has hiccups. He's behind the shack now so I can't see him. I wait, expecting to hear a major crash, but I don't.

"Friends don't let friends drive drunk," I say to the fence post. "But what about people you hate?"

"Shouldn't let them drive either." The voice comes from next to me, and I whip around to look straight into Sunday Boy's blue eyes—not two feet away from me. He leans on the fence rail.

"That black horse probably was a good one a while ago. Too bad he fell into old Floyd's hands. Maybe you should make Floyd an offer and buy that guy."

"Why would I waste good money on a beat up old horse?"

"I dunno. Seems like you got him tucked under your heart."

I gotta look blank. Nobody in this world talks like that.

"That's what my daddy says. When you love something, it's tucked under your heart."

"I don't love one single thing around this place," I say, before I walk away.

"That's gotta be terrible for you," Sunday Boy calls after me.

What is he, anyway, a damned preacher? I scuff the dirt with my feet. "I don't have anything tucked anyplace."

Chapter 18

Shawna

Pollard Nix is my history teacher. He's standing in front of the class, tugging at a really ugly floral tie and looking a lot like a sausage stuffed inside his jacket. He's said something important because he picks up the chalk and turns to write on the board. When he lifts his arm, the stitches along the back seam give way, so now the lining peeks out from inside. It's kind of like looking at a guy's fly that comes unzipped. You want to say, "Hey! It's snowing, bud." But instead, some students slide glances at each other, while others pretend Pollard Nix isn't popping out of his clothes. I join with the last group and write down the dates he's scribbled on the scarred blackboard.

Sweet River High is so far under the hi-tech radar that I'm guessing whiteboard has never been an entry in their dictionaries. The computer lab is the size of maybe a big broom closet, and their computers are charity donations that the good citizens of the community have provided. Three Apples (plain with fat monitors) and two PCs loaded with older Windows software. The third and newest one actually has the latest version. Networking is not in any-one's vocabulary, but that's fine with me. I'm not into being connected with anyone, so I don't bother with the so-called computer lab.

Pollard is making more points . . . important ones. I'm writing—I think. But my head keeps snapping back and waking me up, so maybe I'm actually not awake. I'm dreaming I'm writing. *Snap*. I'm dreaming I'm meeting the Sunday Boy. *Snap*. I'm . . .

"Shawna. Pssst."

Snap.

"He's coming. Wake up."

I look across at The Troll.

"Nix" she hisses. "Look out." She buries her nose in her book and scribbles notes on the lined paper next to it.

"Miss Stone?"

I look up at my friend Pollard Nix and yawn.

"It seems I'm boring you today," he says.

"No." I'm awake now so I can answer and sound alert. "Not today."

"Nice to hear. Please see me at the end of class." He glances at The Troll, who has filled the entire page with . . . what? He walks back to the front of the room, white stuffing poking out even further from his jacket seam than the last time I looked.

The Troll slides me a glance and a grin. *What does she want? Good grief, go away.*

The bell ends my captivity in history, but Pollard wants more of me today, so I gather my books and shuffle to his desk.

He looks up from his seat and smiles. "How about a mini-review, Miss Stone? I think it would do us both good to go over today's lesson."

I shrug and shift my books to my hip. He breaks a pencil.

"What was today's lesson?" he asks, staring at the two pieces of yellow #2 in each hand.

"Industrial Revolution," I reply.

He nods.

"And what are the main points I made today?"

"Children suffered. Some people organized the National Child Labor Committee in 1904. They wanted to stop the abuse of young workers. By 1907, about two million little kids worked and didn't go to school. In 1912, Taft created the Children's Bureau. He gave a woman named Julia Lathrop the job as head of the bureau." I shift my books to my other hip.

Pollard Nix tosses the two pieces of pencil so they popped into the air. Without saying anything, he shoves his chair away from his desk and stands. He walks to the door, stops, and faces me. "And just think what more you could tell me, Miss Stone, if you'd remained awake?"

"There was more?"

He slams the door so hard, the picture of George Washington tilts left.

I wait for the seismic activity to settle, and then I walk out into the hall—smack into The Troll.

"So?" she asks.

I shake my head and walk to my locker. She trails

after me. "I didn't want you to get in trouble. That's why I . . . you know, warned you."

I spin the combination on my locker then turn around. "Look. I think it's grand of you to, like, help me out. Really. But I don't need your help. Put that in your notes. Do not help Shawna. She don't want it! Okay?" I grab my books for English and dump History in their place. When I turn to leave, she's still standing at my side.

"You always need a friend."

Now I do one of Kay's long blinks that screams fed up. *Go take a bath, okay?* I think it, but I don't say it. *Why even bother?* I push past her and head to English.

Mrs. Heady is not giving us an essay today. What, is she like, sick? Alzheimer's erase her lesson plan? The Troll takes her seat and doesn't look at me. We have achieved separation, Houston. But I'm not in the greatest mood after Pollard Nix and his inquisition. I'm so not going to make it through this year.

Now Mrs. Heady is lecturing and writing and lecturing. I'm about over the top with learning, so I doodle until Monster's face stares up at me. He's beginning to look handsome. At least his clothes don't rip apart to reveal their inside secrets. And he's very patient. There's a lot to like about him. If he just didn't pick on me when I'm down, we'd get along better.

"Shawna?" It's Mrs. Heady.

I look up and stare into the faces of half the class turned in my direction. *And they want what?* I crush Monster's face into a ball and wait. *Someone make a move already, 'cause it's not going to be me.*

"Say, 'it's about death,'" The Troll whispers from behind her book.

I close my eyes and say, "it's about death," but it comes out sounding like it's about a pile of crap. When I open my eyes, Mrs. Heady is writing 'death' on the board. What has that to do with anything? I glance at The Troll, who nods and turns her book so I can read the title of the poem the class is discussing.

"Is there another metaphor that you found?" Mrs. Heady asks.

"The carriage," The Troll answers.

"Excellent," Mrs. Heady says while she writes that on the board as well.

I cradle my forehead in both hands and do my best to look like I'm studying the textbook. I read that poem and I hated it. That poet didn't know squat about waiting for death. It's not that way. The bell rings and I'm out of my seat, hurling Monster into the trash and shoving my way out the door.

Chapter 19

Kay

Kay woke to one of those bright October mornings. The sun slanted across the earth and washed it in a golden light that signaled the end of California's Indian Summer. It was the kind of day when Kay loved to take the gray out for a long ride, sit under a tree, and watch the creek slide past. But, yesterday, when Robby Green had called, asking her to come in, he'd sounded urgent. She'd agreed to meet with him at ten this morning.

By a little after ten, she sat in the principal's office across from Shawna's English teacher, Mrs. Heady. Robby sat at the end of the small conference table. Both wore expressions a lot like people sitting in the family section at a funeral.

"We're very concerned, Kay." His voice sounded tight like his throat was cinching down on his words.

Kay folded her hands in front of her on the table. *Here it comes*, she thought. *What has Shawna done, said?*

"Have you seen anything that might signal Shawna is depressed enough to have thoughts of . . . " he cleared his throat, " . . . suicide?" Robby Green spoke the word softly, but it struck her like a blow across the face.

If she'd been standing, Kay knew she would be holding onto something to keep from falling. Yes, he'd sounded serious when he called her yesterday, but she'd come ready to talk about Shawna's language or her antisocial behavior, not suicide!

She shook her head. No. She'd never suspected anything like that. Was she blind? Stupid? Naïve? How can a sixty-four-year-old woman be naïve? Wait. What makes him jump to the idea of suicide when he's dealing with a sixteen-year-old whose emotions roller-coaster hourly?

"Of course, we can't be sure," he continued, "but, ahem . . . well, Shawna's essays . . . are—" he signaled to Mrs. Heady.

Mrs. Heady leaned forward as if she wanted to share a secret. "Mrs. Stone, I've spoken several times with Mr. Green about Shawna's withdrawal and her sullen attitude, and the fact that I see it worsening almost daily." She cleared her throat, "There are adults who haven't experienced what your granddaughter has. I haven't, so I sometimes don't know how to respond to her work." She held out a crumpled piece of paper. "And I don't often retrieve things students toss into the waste basket, but Shawna was in a darker mood than usual on Monday, and I noticed her doodling. She wasn't on task at all, but when I spoke to her, she did go back to work and complete her assignment. When she left class, she threw this away. I . . . well, I had to know what was on this paper."

Kay took the paper and read the scrawled words. "Pity is for the living, envy is for the dead."

Kay knew that quote. She knew it too well. She'd tortured herself with it after Nicholas died. After Peter left. When her life wasn't worth living anymore.

"Monster. Monster. Just a little longer." The note continued.

Underneath these words, Shawna had drawn a ghoulish face with black, pinpoint eyes and a grin filled with razor sharp teeth. Tiny drops of blood dripped from the gaping lips and pooled at the bottom of the paper. It was childish, except for the ugly face. She held it away and leaned back in her chair, suddenly drained of energy, numb all over, like her arms might feel if she'd slept on them.

Kay let the paper fall to the table and buried her face in her hands.

"I'm very sorry. This is a shock, I know. I hesitated to make such an assumption, and kept thinking this could just be a young girl adjusting to her new life and feeling lonely. But we can't take a chance, especially when we have Mrs. Heady's observations about Shawna's increasing withdrawal from social contact. She has no friends, talks to no one, and she barely participates in class. I feel we need to intervene and get Shawna some help, and we need to do it immediately."

Kay couldn't respond. Her mouth seemed full of sand, and the fears she'd struggled to push aside were popping up like shooting-gallery ducks. What if she couldn't handle this troubled sixteen-year-old? What if something happened to this girl while she was taking care of her? She wasn't even her legal guardian. What if she failed as a grandmother the way she had as a mother? As a wife?

The room closed around her. She was suffocating. She shoved her chair back, walked to the window, and pushed it open. Leaning out, she inhaled the Indian Summer air as though it was her last breath.

She'd learned to value her life, but it wasn't until she'd gone down to the mat with death that she'd learned to truly appreciate it.

U

It had taken Kenny Fargo, a derelict cowboy with more common sense than any man she'd ever met, to put her back into balance. He'd stood in her office door that morning, his grimy hat in his hand. Ten years ago? That long? Yes. A half-hour before, she'd watched Peter drive off down the rutted road for the last time.

"So you're gonna bail out on us, I see." Kenny set the crease in his hat like it was the most important thing he had on his mind at the moment.

"Go away!" she shouted.

"Sure. I can do that real easy. What do you want me to do with the body? How about your horses?"

She looked up at him. The skinny, brown-toothed old devil was grinning at her. And here she was, sitting with a shotgun propped up against the floor and aimed at her chest. What was so funny?

"Seems to me you ought to have thought all that out before you settled yourself down to do what it is you're planning. If I was you, I'd put your wishes down in writing and give them to me before you get on with this little drama."

Kay laid the gun across her desk. "Little drama," she repeated, slumping back in her desk chair. She looked up at Kenny, who was leaning against the doorjamb like he'd dropped in for a Sunday visit. "It would be little, wouldn't it?"

"Afraid, so. Of course, you'd sure have showed him, right? Well, you put down what you want, and I'll do it." He pushed away from the door and took a step back. "Oh, and you have to take the safety off if you want that gun to fire."

U

She pulled the window closed and returned to her seat across from Robby Green. He no longer resembled her grade school chum or the high school president she'd sat beside and tutored through algebra. And for that she was grateful. She could pretend they didn't know each other as she faced him, her privacy stripped, her fear exposed. "What do you suggest I do?"

He reached across and put his hands over hers. "I have several possible sources for help, and we'll work with you, too, so you won't be alone dealing with this crisis."

"Shawna has English next period. Do you want me to send her here?" Mrs. Heady asked.

"Give Mrs. Stone and me some time to go over options. Send her after class." He scribbled on a pink pad and handed Mrs. Heady the small slip of paper.

Mrs. Heady rose, came around the table, and stopped next to Kay. "She's such a bright girl. I know we can help her get through this."

Kay looked at their two faces, so different from each other in all ways except for the tightness around their mouths and the deep creases in their foreheads. She could only imagine what her face must look like. The *Titanic* had just run into the iceberg.

Chapter 20

Shawna

"Hey, Shawna!"

I look behind me. The Sunday Boy with the great jeans is coming my way. *Now what?* I should pretend I don't hear him, but like a jerk I've made eye contact already. I lean against my locker and watch him as he weaves his way through students on their way to class.

He looks just like he does every Sunday—T-shirt with rolled sleeves and the same kind of jeans. He's a head taller than most of the guys in the hall, and seems older than the others in his senior class. *Is it the way he clutches his books in the crook of his arm? The easy way he walks or looks directly into people's eyes when he speaks to them? What do I like about him besides the way his clothes fit? Wait, like him? Not in this lifetime.*

"Guess you're in a hurry," he says, standing in front of me.

"Why?"

"You passed me like someone late for a date. Didn't you see me?"

"I wasn't looking at anybody. I've got English in a couple of minutes." I put a hard edge on my voice like I used to when Mom came home with a new *friend* for me to meet.

"You're not easy to talk to. Do you know that?"

"Never had any complaints before."

"Right."

"Now that you've got my attention, what do you want?" I work at sounding nicer than before, but it doesn't happen.

"Nothing. See you next Sunday." He walks down the hall and steps into a classroom before I realize I have my mouth open to say something.

"Hell with you." I twist the combination on my locker, grab my English book, and slam the tinny door. *Get to English and forget Sunday Boy.*

I can write an essay on the bazillion reasons I hate guys, but do I have the time to waste? I edge into my seat and lean back. My goal today is to count the ceiling tiles, a simple multiplication problem, but Mrs. Heady is not her usual five minutes late, so I pull myself up and prepare to plow my way through another of her essays.

She starts the class, and then patrols the aisles. When she walks down my aisle, she hands me a hall pass.

"You can take care of this at the end of class today."

The Troll shoots me one of her ferret-looks, but I stare her down. She has no idea who she's dealing with yet, but if she keeps it up I'm going to show her.

"Please come to the Principal's office after English today. R. Green."

Now what? I haven't done anything.

The Troll is craning her neck to see what's on the paper. I shoot her a killer look, and she bends over her paper so far her nose almost touches it. I fold the pass and stick it into my notebook.

My essay is lame. I'm too busy thinking about why Mr. Roly-Poly Principal Green wants me in his office.

I've been clean since I came here. Mostly because there isn't much choice. This place squeaks—no grime, no crime.

At the break, I dump my books in my locker and walk into Mr. Green's office as though there's nothing unusual in my visit—as if I do it everyday. But right away I wish for unusual, because awful is what greets me.

Mr. Green, looking like a funeral director, closes the door and pulls out a chair for me. I sit down like that chair has electrical wires attached.

"Shawna, I'm going to show you something, and then I'm going to ask you a difficult question." Mr. Green shoves a piece of crumpled paper across the table. "Is this yours?"

The picture of Monster's face stares up at me. I lean back in my chair, cross my arms, and wait.

"Your grandmother has told me how you came to Sweet River and a little about your life before."

Kay doesn't know anything about my life. She doesn't know anything about me at all, so what's this crap he's spewing?

"How do you feel about being here?"

I shrug. "It's okay."

"What does that mean, exactly?" Mr. Green is pulling out his principal language. Principals sound a lot like cops when they're mining for information.

What does it mean? I don't know what it means. It means okay. I get food. I sleep in a bedroom with a door and in a real bed. Everybody that comes to Kay's is somebody she's known since the earth formed. I haven't seen a cop in a month. I work my butt off, but I'm getting used to it. I have a dog, sort of, and sheep and horses. You know, it's okay.

Aloud I say, "It's regular."

He nods. "And are you happy, living with your grandmother?"

Oh, this is way bad. *Am I happy? Happy is not in my dictionary. I don't feel too edgy at Kay's. I get along with Kenny Fargo okay now, and that Sunday Boy . . . what is his name anyway? I'm getting used to horses and Buster's flea epidemics. I don't even mind those sheep, now that their fur or hair or whatever they have is starting to grow back.*

Aloud I say, "Yes." At the same time I make two fists and jam my hands onto my lap to keep them steady.

Tell him what he wants to hear, Shawna.

Is that Monster? At school? Damn!

"I'm concerned about a couple of things," Mr. Green drowns out Monster. "When I look at your face you don't seem to be listening. Are you somewhere else?"

That is one stupid question. I'm in your office, sitting in an electric chair across from a nosey fat man. I've got Monster skulking around here someplace, and you want me to answer something that's totally obvious.

Aloud I say, "I guess I'm just surprised by your questions. Maybe that's why I look the way I do." *I wish I could see how I look right now. Where's Tuan's mirror when you need it?* I shift in my seat and tuck my hands under my butt. That helps.

"Well, then about this drawing. Tell me about it." He pushes my picture of Monster across the desk.

No. It's nobody's business.

You tell him, Shawna. Monster's still lurking.

"Sorry about that. I had an argument with this guy just before class and I was really upset. That's a picture of him."

Oh, Shawna, you are good, Monster croons.

"So when Mrs. Heady noticed you were in a dark mood, it was about this argument?"

"Yeah."

"Dark moods can be scary."

This is going nowhere. I'm not talking about my moods. They're mine, and they're private. Mrs. Nose-in-My-Business Heady can butt out, and so can you, Mr. Principal.

"Sorry she's worried. I'll try to leave the moods outside class. Everything's fine with me, really. I guess I just have to get used to a new school and a new way of doing things."

Does he buy that? Yes. He looks like bricks fell off his head. He's smiling at me, and that tight muscle near his right eye isn't twitching now. I'd finally said something to get him off my case.

"Thank you for being so open with me. Just remember you can always come in and talk whenever you need someone to listen. I'm a good listener, Shawna." Mr. Green stands.

I crush Monster's face between my hands. He slinks away.

Chapter 21

Kay

Kay tightened her clenched hands around the steering wheel of the old truck, waiting for Shawna to walk out the front door of the school. Had Robby asked the questions they'd agreed on? How had Shawna answered them?

Kay leaned back in the seat and tried to imagine the meeting in the principal's office. How Shawna's dark eyes would shift away before every response. How her voice would sound when she'd answer her usual, "It's okay." How she'd shrug her shoulders and, for that matter, her whole being. *The girl didn't care about anything. And how could someone only sixteen years old not care about something? Her whole life lay in front of her!*

When Robby asked how she felt about living here, Kay could hear Shawna's mind churning: *I hate that ranch. I might as well be on Mars. I hate living with an old man and an old woman, cleaning up after horses everyday except Sunday. And let me tell you how fun Sundays are around that place.*

The next question made Kay's knuckles ache, she gripped the wheel so hard.

"And are you happy, living with your grandmother?"

Shawna might shrug again or say yes, but she'd think: *My grandmother's a cranky old witch who's on my case from sun up 'till I hit the sack. What's to be happy about?*

That's what Shawna's shrug—what her yes really meant. And she wasn't too far wrong. Kay knew she was cranky, but she didn't know any other way to be. She'd grown into who she was over the years, and now, when she looked back to find how she'd gotten to this place in her life, she'd forgotten most of the journey, and she couldn't remember how she used to be. She could only remember the beginning. The day Peter stood in the doorway, suitcase in hand, face set in that expression he wore when he wanted to cry but refused. He was hurting and she was dying, but neither of them had the energy or the desire to reach out to the other.

He was leaving.

She was staying.

Their son was dead and their marriage had died along with him. End of one story. Beginning of another: her journey to cranky old witch.

Where did Shawna live all day, all night? Robby Green knew from only two conversations with her that she often was someplace other than the present. And Shawna was never surprised by anything. Angry, yes. In fact, while Kay thought about the exchange that was going on that very moment between Shawna and Robby, she realized the only emotion Shawna had ever expressed in front of her was anger. *At least that was something*, she thought. *At least one ball she hit came back. Shawna never shrugged when she was angry.*

How would Shawna handle the issue of her dark moods? She'd come up with some reasonable explanation for them. She was good at lying, but Kay was good at hearing lies and seeing through them for what they were. Too many years around Kenny Fargo and horses had done that for her, she guessed. There was no time or patience for lies as far as any of those wonderful creatures were concerned.

Robby Green hadn't had the privilege of attending the Kenny Fargo School of Life, so Shawna would be able to lead him right where she wanted him.

At least Robby had given Kay some options. He could refer her to others who were more qualified to deal with Shawna's problems than he was. The district had a psychologist he could bring in. There were several psychologists and therapists in Sacramento he could recommend. There was a teen crisis hotline, and he would give Kay that number. But she'd have to make the final decision about which way to go.

He'd insisted she leave the room while he talked to Shawna, but she'd refused. "I don't care about good counseling techniques, Robby," she'd said, "I'm staying right here. You do your job. I'll do mine."

"Kay, you have to trust me on this one. I promise to share anything I think you need to know to help your granddaughter, but she won't talk freely in front of both of us."

She'd let him talk her into leaving. Another mistake?

U

At the sound of the truck door opening, Kay sat up. Shawna, her jaw clenched, climbed into the passenger seat and slammed the door.

"How did it go with the principal?"

"It didn't."

"What do you mean?" *Maybe she hadn't talked to him. Why not? Robby said he'd see her right after her English period.* "You didn't talk to him?"

Shawna looked out the passenger window as if Kay hadn't spoken to her.

For heaven sakes at least answer me. "You're upset. Can I help?"

"No." Shawna's voice was as empty as the expression she turned on Kay.

Please open up to me. Please let me in. Kay wanted to say it, but instead she turned the key in the ignition and shifted into low.

Chapter 22

Shawna

After Robby Green's pathetic counseling session I feel like a dishrag someone's wrung out. I climb into Kay's truck, and when I look at my reflection in her rearview mirror, I'm surprised I'm not in a twist.

"How did it go with the principal?"

Well how in the hell does she think it went? Mr. Mush Mouth yammered at me. I smiled and tried to give him the answers he wanted. Monster showed up to lend a hand. Thank you very much. "It didn't."

"You didn't talk to him?"

I talked at him. He talked at me. I wish she'd stop interrogating me. I've had it with people nosing into my life.

"You're upset. Can I help?"

Help me with what, Grandma? Just what is it you think you can help me with? "No."

Kay looks away, then back with her seat-belt stare. She starts the truck and pulls out of the parking lot without another word. Interrogation over.

After she passes the turnoff to the ranch she says, "I

have an errand before we go home. I didn't get to Max's Rural Supply today."

Her icebreakers would not stand up at parties. I shrug and guess she sees me out of the corner of her eye because her knuckles whiten on the steering wheel.

Rural Supply is the ranchers' supermarket. There's hay, and oats, and horse blankets in all sizes and colors. While Kay puts together her order, I roam the aisles and read the labels. Something to do, at least, while I'm stuck here. When I get to the vitamin section, it occurs to me that Drunk Floyd's black horse might benefit from a vitamin boost. Kenny gives Kay's horses vitamins all the time, so I search the shelves for a bottle that looks familiar, like what Kenny keeps in his leather bag.

And there it is. Very big and . . . and almost my week's allowance. There's no way I'm spending that kind of money to buy horse vitamins.

I walk away.

Still there's that black horse . . . I see him next to Floyd's ratty barn, head high, not like the others that have already given up and stare at the ground, waiting to die. He's got hope somewhere inside him.

He's a horse, Shawna. Too stupid to know there is no hope.

Kay's still talking with the guy at the counter, so I go back to the vitamins. It's been a while since I lifted something. I feel that old tingle when I wrap my fingers around the plastic bottle and take it down from the shelf. Remember what Mom showed you, okay?

Read the label.

Put the bottle back.

Take another one down.

Read.

Put this one back, but at the same time shove the first one up your sleeve. Even the surveillance cameras have a hard time seeing that maneuver.

Now stroll.

Take your time.

Look at other stuff.

Never rush.

Start for the door.

Turn back and look at something else.

Mom's voice: "Think, I've got all the time in the world."

"Shawna?" It's Kay.

"Coming." I'm so obedient.

Chapter 23

Shawna

I name the black horse Magic. I once read a novel about a kid named Magic. He made it out of the slums and into big-league baseball, even after beatings left him with a gimpy leg. The kid had real guts to go from being crippled to being one of the best runners on the team. It was just a story, but I liked it.

Magic doesn't exactly run to meet me when I climb over the fence and onto Drunk Floyd's property, but at least he doesn't keep his distance like he used to. He sidles up slowly and noses my pockets for the apples I have tucked inside. The other two still hang back, but I know they'll come around as soon as they get a taste of what Magic's enjoying.

I wait until Drunk Floyd's car disappears down the road, then climb the fence and drop down into enemy territory. It's another dynamic Sunday on the ranch, and Floyd always goes into town Sunday, so that's the day I have Magic to myself for a few hours.

Today I'm armed with the vitamins I lifted last week

when Kay hauled me to Rural Supply. I've seen Kenny dose Kay's horses with these giant pills, and her horses are buffed critters, so I figure this bony old guy needs a power boost and these pills might help.

From Kay's barn I grab a pan and some of the gray's special grain. In the bottom of the pan, I mash the pills like I've seen Kenny do, and then stir the powder in water; next I pour in the grain. Magic scarfs it all down and noses the apple chunks out of my hand. I reach up and touch the white patch on his forehead. He jerks his head back and snorts, like he's saying, "Hands off!"

I wait until he comes up close again for more apple, and then I stroke the same spot. He shakes his head, but he doesn't back away this time.

"You'll get used to me. Just like I'm getting used to you and all your cousins around this place."

I'm concentrating so hard on getting close to Magic that I don't hear the car coming. When the door slams, it's too late to hide. Drunk Floyd is stomping across the pasture toward me. Magic and the other horses vanish around the side of the barn.

"I'm calling the sheriff unless you get off my property and stay off!" he shouts.

"I just wanted—"

"You deaf?"

"You sober?" I yell back.

I figure he probably is sober for a change, so now I don't have the advantage I usually do. But I'm faster than he is, so instead of trying to reason with the old crab, I sprint to the fence and hurtle over it to the other side.

"And you stay the hell over there, you hear?" He waves his fist in my direction, and I consider flipping him off, but change my mind. I'll get him sometime when he's staggering all over the place.

"That was some scene." Sunday Boy is leaning on the rake and smiling at me from the barn.

"Yeah. He's a piece of work, that guy."

"What are you doing over there, anyway?"

I almost come back with, "What's it to you?" But I change my mind. "The horses. I sneak over once in a while and give them something."

He nods. "Well, I got work to do. See you around."

"Wait!" That comes out before I think. Now that he's looking at me, I have to come up with something to say. "I don't know your name."

"Nope. You don't." He goes inside the barn.

I scuff my way inside after him. "What is it?"

"Casey."

"I'm only asking because I can't call you Sunday Boy all the time."

"Oh, yeah? I didn't know you called me anything at all."

Why do I care about his name? Why am I even bothering to talk to him?

He hooks the lead to the gray and brings her outside, where he ties her off. I stand back as he paints some smelly ointment all over her feet and then soaps her front to back with warm suds. He hoses her down and scrapes the water off her front, sides, and rear. Then he dries her legs with a towel. So many steps, and he's careful with each one, like what he's doing is the most important job in the world. He works on horses a lot like Kenny does, and the gray stands easy under his hands. She trusts him, knows she's safe. I watch while he pulls a mask over her face and sprays her with some stuff that Kenny says helps keep the flies away. When he finishes, he turns her out to pasture, to have her Sunday the way she wants it.

Another question bubbles to the surface before I can stop it. "Have you always worked with horses?"

"Since I could walk. We still have a couple, but my dad had to sell some off. Too expensive." He looks down at me. "How about you?"

"Never. Well, not until I came here."

"You're lucky you're here. Kay's got a nice place and her boarders take good care of their horses. Not like over there." He nods toward Drunk Floyd's. "Nobody does anything for those guys. I expect they'll end up in Texas one of these days."

"Not my favorite state." I remember that week in Houston and the motel from hell with armor-plated cockroaches scuttling in the dark corners. After Mom turned the lights off, their beetle legs clicked across the linoleum, coming to get me under the sheets. I stole a flashlight the first chance I got, and every night I shined it down the side of my bed. It still grosses me out to think about them creeping across my toes on my way to pee.

"It won't be those horses' favorite state either."

It's the way he says it that sounds creepy and makes me want to know what he means. I chew on the inside of my mouth before I ask, "Why won't they like Texas? I did-n't think horses cared where they lived."

"Oh, they won't live there long. A few days maybe. A while back they'd have ended up in a can for Buster's din-ner. Now I think they ship the meat to Canada or Europe."

Horse in a can! I'm glad he's walking into the tack room and hasn't stopped to look at me. It's like I've sud-denly shown up naked in public and have nowhere to hide. If I'd been in front of Tuan's mirror, I'd have seen the face Monster always sees, fear scribbled all over it.

I have to put my head down between my knees or I know I'm going to topple over. My stomach's a washer going into an out-of-kilter spin, my head has a rope cinched tight around it and it throbs. When I stand up again, I look across at Drunk Floyd's.

Magic pokes his head through the rails, looking at me, waiting for me to come to him.

I take a few steps toward him. *No. Stop.*

"I can't waste my time on you anymore," I yell. "You're horse meat on the hoof."

My voice must sound different to him, because he ducks out from between the rails and shambles away.

"Magic. I . . . Forget it. You're history, so why waste my time?" I start toward the house.

"Do you say mean things to everyone and every-thing?" Casey calls after me.

"What's it to you?" I look over my shoulder.

He shakes his head and goes back into the barn.

I see more of his back than anything else. Jerk.

Chapter 24

Shawna

One cool thing about Sweet River High is the wide grassy spot with the big trees and picnic tables. Everybody calls it The Park. As long as the weather stays good, lots of kids eat lunch or hide behind the tree trunks, sucking on each other's face. Mr. Green gets his exercise every noon, pulling lips apart.

I spot him heading my way and bury my nose in my English Lit book.

"Afternoon, Shawna," Mr. Green calls.

I nod, hunching over my book.

"I see you're enjoying the last of our sunny days." Mr. Green never takes hints. He's the kind of guy Mom says you have to hit up the side of the head.

"Yeah." I give him my go-away-you-jerk look.

"I talked to your grandmother again yesterday. She says you're going to a therapist in Sacramento next week."

I shrug. "I guess."

"I'm pleased to hear that. I'll check back with you to see how things go, all right?"

"Whatever."

The shrink is Kay's idea, not mine. And I'm not going along with the program. She can make all the appointments she wants, but making me talk is totally not happening. I have Monster under control. I can manage anything, so take your shrink and stuff him.

I lean back against the tree and flip to Chapter Four, The Romantic Movement. On the first page is a picture of a guy on a black horse, galloping after another guy who is freaked out because the guy chasing him is headless! This is romantic?

"What are you doing?" Casey sits down on the grass next to me.

"What does it look like?"

"You never let up, do you?"

I close the book. "What's that supposed to mean?"

"It means that you are the hardest egg I've ever met."

I laugh. "I've never been called an egg before."

"You outta laugh more." He stands to leave. "You look nice when you do, Shawna."

Nice. Me? That's interesting. Shawna and nice in the same sentence from the guy who—damn it—has the greatest butt I've ever seen. Let it go, girlfriend. You have enough on your plate without this . . . this perfectly handsome guy who has just turned his back and is walking away. "How come you're always walking off in the middle of a conversation?"

"This is a conversation?" He smiles over his shoulder. "I thought it was just another chance for you to show me how tough you are. I'll see you later about what I came to say."

"Whatever!" I slam my book on the ground.

"See? Shawna, the hardest egg around." He waves and walks over to join a group of students sitting at one of the picnic tables.

He doesn't know tough. I'll show him tough one of these days. I pick up my book and find my place, but Mrs. Heady's assignment doesn't seem as interesting as it did a minute ago. I hold the book so I look like I'm reading, but I watch over the top. Who's he talking to? Two girls I don't know sitting on top of the table. One is arched back, her boobs pushed to the sky. And on the bench is . . . Oh, my gawd. It's The Troll! He's talking to old ferret-face.

I snap the book closed and stand up. That's all I can take. I walk directly to the picnic table and tap Casey on the shoulder. "I just wanted to conclude our *conversation*. Don't even come near me anymore. You smell like troll, and troll is a turn-off."

"Who is she?" The blond with the boobs asks.

When I look at her and then at the other girl next to her, I choke. They look exactly alike.

The Troll mumbles something about my being a new student.

"What's your problem?" one twin asks.

"Hold on, Deanna." Casey says, and he turns to face me. "I get to ask that question. What *is* your problem, Shawna?"

"I don't have a problem as long as you stay away from me. Your present company stinks, and I don't want it to rub off on me." I look at the twins and at The Troll. "Spell stink with a capital *S*." I leave them all with their mouths open.

I cram the books I don't need for my next class into my locker and go to the girls' room. When I come out, Casey is propped against the opposite wall with his arms crossed over his chest.

"Hold up," he says.

I stop a few feet away and face him. "Guess you don't hear too well. I told you—"

Casey steps toward me. "I hear better than you think. I hear a city freak wise ass trying to out shout a cornered kid. If you can't hate it, you're afraid of it. How close am I?"

Our eyes lock onto each other. The end-of-lunch bell rings, and kids pour around us like we're boulders in a river current.

"I'll meet you after school today. We got business to take care of." He pushes past me, brushing my shoulder with his hand.

"Business? What's that supposed—?" He's already down the hall. I shiver, but I'm not getting my old shakes. This is totally different.

Chapter 25

Shawna

That afternoon at the end of class, I jump from my seat before the bell stops and push out of the door ahead of students who sit in the front of the room. I run to the exit and take the steps two at a time.

I already have one shrink in my future and don't want Casey, the wanna-be shrink, coming down on my head about the two sides of me he hears whenever I talk to him. The air is warm. A breeze whips dried leaves into little tornados across the lawn, and I think about what winter might be like in Sweet River. That reminds me, Kay's talking about more shopping. *Gawd!* And the word *parka* crept into the conversation, so I already see myself wadded up in an Eskimo suit.

"Escaping?"

I don't have to turn around. I know Casey's voice. "I have to meet Kay." I try to look busy, searching for Kay's truck.

"I told her I'd pick you up and bring you home today. Hop in."

It has to be a conspiracy, Sweet River against Shawna. "Why? And who do you think you are, anyway?"

"The guy with the wheels who's going to get you the six miles to Kay's ranch."

He wouldn't look so smug if I hauled off and socked him in the jaw, something I consider while gritting my teeth to keep from telling him to get lost. But six miles is one hell of a hike. I swing my backpack off my shoulder and walk to the curb. He stands next to his black Chevy pickup and holds open the passenger door. His truck looks a lot better than Kay's. It's clean inside and out, and the upholstery doesn't look like a cat has shredded it.

With his free hand, he ushers me inside and closes the door. When he climbs in the driver seat and starts the engine, he looks at me.

"What?"

"Seat belt."

Does every driver in this place follow DMV seat-belt rules one hundred percent of the time? I pull the belt around myself and shove the buckle into the clasp.

When I look out, The Troll is on the lawn, watching. I close my eyes as we sweep past. But I think she waves as we go by. *Is she dim? Or is she like a dog that always noses people who hate dogs? What do I have to do to keep her and her stench away from me?*

Once in the cab, Casey doesn't say anything. And I'm so used to not talking when Kay comes to pick me up that I don't even notice. I do notice that he doesn't take the turnoff to the ranch, and instead drives into Sweet River, where he pulls up in front of Rural Supply and gets out.

"Come on." He opens the passenger door and waits for me to climb down.

"Why are we going in here?"

"I told you, business. Do you have some money?" He walks inside the store and leaves me standing by the truck.

"Money?" I follow him into the store. He's at the counter, talking to the guy Kay says owns the place. *Max? Moe? Something with an M.*

"Shawna." Casey calls. "You know Max, right?"

I nod.

"He has your bill ready. You got twenty on you?"

What's he talking about? I narrow my eyes, knowing something is coming down and I'm not going to like it. *Take it head on. Look like you know what this is about.* I walk to the counter and open my backpack. I've tucked Kenny's generous salary, all of twenty a week, into the outside pocket. I pull it out and drop it on the counter.

Max gives me fifteen cents in change, writes on a piece of paper, and shoves it across to me, saying, "Account settled. Next time I'd appreciate your paying when you take the merchandise."

I don't look at him or the paper, but I fold it in half and stuff it into my backpack, along with my change.

"I'm sure she'll do that. Right, Shawna?"

I swing my backpack over one shoulder and pretend I didn't hear.

"Bye, Max. See you next week when I pick up Kay's order," Casey says. Then he puts his hand at my back and pushes me out the door. "Come on, Shawna, I'll buy you a Coke now that you're down to your last fifteen cents!"

I can't believe it. He's laughing at me.

"I don't drink Coke." I climb into the truck and stare out the side window.

"Then I'll buy you a 7-Up."

"I don't—"

"Then you can watch me drink!" He steps on the gas a little hard and we squeal away from Rural Supply.

How did Casey find out about the vitamins? This is the first time I've ever been caught, and it has to be by a guy named Max in Podunk Sweet River and a Sunday Boy. I must be slipping.

The café in Sweet River reminds me of an old movie set. Brick walls and ruffled curtains are the main decorations. The tables wobble under red-and-white checked cloths, and when I pull out a chair, flakes of four different paint layers come off on my hand. Casey orders a Coke and a glass of water with a lemon slice on the side. When the waitress brings our order, he squeezes the lemon slice into the water and shoves the glass in front of me. "I don't want your sour level to go down."

Before I can push up from the table, he has me by my wrist and I can't move.

"What is wrong with you?" I say between gritted teeth.

"That's the question I keep asking you, remember? And I'm not the only one around school who's asking it." He sips his Coke, but holds onto my wrist like a rein on a runaway horse. "What *is* wrong with you, Shawna? The first day I saw you from the barn, I thought you looked like someone I'd like to know. I've tried to talk to you

every time I see you, to let you know who I am. And you
. . . you're plain nasty in return."

"It's my middle name. Now do you mind letting the
blood back into my hand?"

He lets go and sits back, staring at me. "Okay. I'm
finished."

He goes to the cash register and pays the check. Without looking back, he opens the door and walks out to his
truck. He starts the engine and waits until I get in and click
my seat belt in place, but he never looks at me or speaks
until we reach Kay's.

"End of the line," he says, when he pulls to a stop at
the house.

I climb out and hold the door open. "End of the line,"
I repeat. "Are you a prophet *and* a psychologist, Casey?"

"I'm neither one, but I'll tell you this, if you lift something from Max's again, he'll go to the cops. Max has his
eye on you, and I'm not running interference for you
again."

I glance toward the barn, where Kay is working a
horse on a line in the open arena.

"Kay doesn't know," he says, and before I can close
the door on the truck, he reaches across and slams it. He
does a one-eighty in the driveway and tears down the rutted road, a brown comet trailing behind.

129

Chapter 26

Shawna

Sunday, again! Arrrg! In Sweet River there are more Sundays than any other day of the week, I swear. I decide that instead of staying at the ranch to watch the manure pile heat up, I'll hitch a ride into Sweet River and do a little exploring on my own. It's like decades since I've had some time without Kay or Kenny riding herd on me.

See? You're even starting to think like them, Shawna.

I get up early before Kenny comes to the house and before Kay makes her coffee. I say adios to Buster, who needs a few rocks thrown his way before he gets the picture and turns around. Then I walk down to the main road. I no sooner stick out my thumb than a truck pulls to a stop and the man hooks his thumb at me to jump in. *Cool.*

"Where you off to, honey?" he asks.

"Just to town for a few hours." I use the voice that always distracted tourists while Mom lifted their wallets.

"Where d'ya live?"

"Down there." I point toward Kay's. "You know Kay Stone?"

"No. Can't recall that name," he says.

Everybody for twenty miles knows my grandmother, so right here I think, *you should get out, now*. But do I? No. It's Sunday, a day that's longer than a freight train. I've got nothing but escape on my mind.

We pull into Sweet River, and the man asks me to join him for coffee.

"I'm buying, sweetheart. You can't pass up a free cup of java, right?"

To give myself a little credit for not being entirely loopy, I check inside the café and see four people inside. I figure there's safety in numbers. I shrug. "Sure."

So by nine o'clock, I'm sitting at one of the wobbly tables, my elbows on red-and-white checkered plastic, sipping coffee. He orders waffles, but I stick with coffee and turn down food.

"So, Shawna, what's a pretty young thing such as yourself doing in Sweet River?" The waitress brings his waffles and he buries them under butter pats and an inch of syrup. He cuts off big chunks of the fried dough and stuffs them into his mouth. When he chews he smacks his lips and syrup seeps out and slides down his chin.

I make up a story. "I'm visiting my grandmother while my mother tours Europe in a Shakespearean play." His eyes glaze a bit on the Shakespearean reference, and I smile.

I stop smiling when I feel his hand slide up my knee.

I'm on my feet so fast that the people sitting near us jump and look under their tables to see if something is crawling across the floor.

"Oh, come on. Sit down," the man says, licking his lips and slugging down the last of his coffee. "I was just being friendly."

"I don't do friendly," I say. I'm at the door and pulling it open. The glass panes rattle when I shut it behind me, and my insides rattle the same way.

Stupid! Stupid! I clench my fists and take a deep breath. Sweet River has a population of eight hundred and sixty-one. Eight hundred and fifty-nine people are like Kay and Kenny, but do I hitch a ride into town with any of them? Noooo. I get the one pervert in town.

In Las Vegas, I'm a cat. I can slink along the wall so nobody sees me if I don't want them to, and I never get caught by some skank jumping out of the alley and grabbing me like I always read about in the newspapers. Nobody's going to stuff me into the trunk of a car! But what just happened is pathetic. Sweet River is acting like tenderizer. I'm getting soft—Sweet River soft.

I burn where he touched me, five fat fingers spread across my knee and I have to get it off. I pull up my jeans, spit into my hand and rub on the place, but it's a brand and it's getting hotter. I'm freaking. The shakes are bubbling to the surface.

I look both ways along the main street. A drugstore, a market, a hardware line up to my left. The Sweet River barbershop, a bank, and the fire station are on my right, and if I go in that direction, I'll wind up on the highway back to Kay's. Straight across the street is a grassy area with a plastic slide and a couple of rusty swings. A narrow street circles up from the main one and winds up the hill behind the park, so I cross over and climb the hill, thinking that at least I can get out of the old pervert's line of sight.

I reach the top of the first turn in the road and look back on the grassy park and across at the café. His truck is still parked in front.

Still stuffing his fat face.

I turn and walk up farther, until I can't see the town anymore. I come to what I guess is the residential part of Sweet River, but the houses look more like small rooms, leaning every which way like crooked teeth. They're tucked under trees and behind shrubs that nobody's hacked back since the last century, so I can only see a door or a window, and sometimes a corner of a place peeking through branches.

I have to duck where the vines or the tree limbs dangle low over the road, and I keep tripping on roots that bulge out of the dirt.

I didn't plan on a hike!

I should go back down, but I don't want to run into old waffle lips again. I'll give him enough time to eat the café out of supplies; then I'll head back to the highway and hitch a ride to Kay's. *I need water. I have to wash my knee. I have to wash the coffee out of my mouth. I have . . . The shakes. I've got 'em now. Can't stop. Keep walking. That usually helps.*

I look into the yards as I pass, until I find one with a hose hooked to a spigot in the front. I turn on the faucet and hose off my knee. I don't care if my jeans get soaked.

I gulp the cold hose water, spit, and douse my face. When I look up, I about drop my upper teeth.

"Hi, Shawna."

It's The Troll. She's standing on the front steps, looking at me.

I put the hose down and back away. "Sorry. I was thirsty. I didn't know I was taking your water."

"It's like all the other water around here. It won't kill you just because it comes out of my hose."

"No. I didn't mean it that way. I just—"

"I know what you mean."

I really hate it when someone says that to me. Nobody knows what I mean unless I tell them, and I'm not telling her a thing!

"Thank you for the water. That's what I mean and nothing else." *Great, Shawna. You went and told her what you mean and you just said you weren't going to do that. What's wrong with you?*

"If you're not scared to come inside, I can give you cold water in a glass." The Troll leans against the doorjamb. "The glass is clean."

"I never said it wasn't!"

She laughs. I've never seen her do anything except stare at me or whisper warnings, and now she stands there laughing!

"You don't have to say it, Shawna. Who knows, maybe I read minds." She turns to go inside, and then looks back. "Coming?"

Today is not working out as I'd planned. First I get a ride from a fat-handed freak, and then I get cornered by my high school troll buddy. Man, I shoulda stayed home and watched the Sunday Boys. No, I can't do that anymore. Casey might stab me with a pitchfork.

I follow her inside.

I swear, the house is smaller and darker than a broom closet, and marbles would roll into the back corners of the living room if you put them in the center of the floor. I feel like I'm visiting Puzzle World, where nothing's actually level.

"Come into the kitchen." The Troll calls from the other room, and I back through the doorway, still trying to make sense of the living room. When I turn, she's holding out a glass of water. "This house is really old."

"How old?"

"A hundred and fifty years. All of them are about the same on this road. Miners built rooms to live in during the Gold Rush. Other people came later and added on to them."

I drink the water and give her back the glass.

"More?" she asks.

I shake my head.

"You want to see my room?" The Troll doesn't wait for me to answer. She presses past me, back into the living room and turns right, down a short, narrow hall.

I duck my head and fold my arms across my chest before I follow her. The low door and ceiling make me feel like a giant.

Her room is big and it has light from windows along the back wall. The bed is small but neat, and covered with a pink flowered bedspread and one pink pillow. *The Troll in pink. Who would have thought?* Her desk stands against the opposite wall, and it shines from so much polishing that the dark, sleek wood reflects my face.

"Nice." I'm trying to get over what I'm seeing. The Troll has a great room. "How long have you lived here?"

"Ten years. My mom has a job at the bank. It's close, so she can walk to work. Saves money on gas."

"You and your mom live alone?" *Not that I'm really interested.*

She nods. "My dad left before I was born."

"Uh-huh." I could add stuff about my dad, but I don't. *Keep to yourself, Shawna. Play your hand close. It's the only way to win.* "What's your real name?" I ask before I think how that's going to sound, but she misses the point, and I don't have to walk around the slur.

"Marta. Don't you hear Mrs. Heady all the time? Marta, stand up straight. Marta, go to the board. Marta, do this. Marta, do that."

"Guess I wasn't listening."

"That's what I thought. You're someplace else most of the time." She sits on the edge of her bed. "Sit down." She motions toward the desk chair. "I know you don't like me, but it doesn't really matter. You don't like anybody, so I don't take it personally."

I open my mouth to tell her to stuff it, but instead say, "I'm new, so I don't know all the ropes yet."

"You know a lot more ropes than the rest of us. You've got to. I mean Las Vegas!" Marta laughs like she did before, kind of nervous.

I stand up and almost tip the chair over.

"Hey! I'm not laughing at you. I think you're cool, but you don't give anyone a chance to know you. Maybe if you did, you'd find someone you like, or at least get along with."

"Friends make me nervous." I walk toward the door. "I gotta go. I didn't tell my grandmother where I was going, and she raises all kinds of hell when I break her rules."

Marta follows me to the front yard and onto the road. "See you tomorrow."

I shrug. "Sure." I don't look back, but I swing my hips a little more because I know she's watching me—Shawna, who knows the ropes.

That was weird. I wonder how it'll be in class, when I sit next to her. Will she still give me those ferret looks? Will I have to talk to her? What'll I do if . . . no, not happening.

I reach the grassy park and go left along the main street toward the highway with my thumb out. In about two minutes, a truck stops alongside me. *Oh, no. It's Kay's truck with Kenny driving and Buster in the back.*

"Howdy, Missy!"

"Are we back to Missy?" I climb into the passenger seat.

"Yes, we are, because your grandmother's about ready to thrash your backside from here to Las Vegas and back again for not telling her where you were off to this morning. I sure do hope you got a whopper of a story to settle her down."

137

"I went to see a . . . friend." I never thought that line would pass my lips. Sweet River soft again.

Kenny gives me the *seat-belt stare*; then puts the truck into gear and rolls onto the highway. He looks at me from under his sweat-soaked tan hat. "You got a friend?"

"Sure."

He nods.

I shrug.

Kay meets us at the front of the house, one hand on each hip, her face hard. Even from the truck I can see the red around her eyes. Man, does she look scary.

Chapter 27

Kay

Kay woke that Sunday to the sound of Buster whining. She pulled her curtain aside and looked out. Why was that dog running down the road then back? She opened the window and whistled. Buster ran to the porch and pawed the front door until she let him in.

She made coffee, finished her bookkeeping and by nine was caught up.

Kenny had already taken up his spot on the porch, but Shawna hadn't come out of her room yet.

Kay tapped on Shawna's bedroom door. She waited, listening, then looked inside. Shawna's bed was empty. Kay went to the kitchen and filled her empty coffee cup and looked outside, but the backyard was empty. "Shawna?" She called from the back door and waited. When Shawna didn't poke her head out of the barn, Kay pulled on her boots and walked across to Floyd's. Maybe she had gone to see the black horse.

Floyd's horses were grazing at the back of his property, but Shawna was nowhere in sight. Kay walked back to her barn and checked the stalls, then returned to the house, where Kenny had already taken up his post on the front porch with his Sunday paper.

"She's not at Floyd's. She's not in the barn or in her room." Kay paced the length of the porch and back.

"Now settle down. She's around here someplace." But he folded the paper and dropped it next to the rocker.

Kay's mind spun with all the possibilities of where Shawna might have taken off to, but with each step, she felt her heart thud harder against her chest. *What if she's run away? What if she's on her way back to Las Vegas? She could be hurt. She could be lost. After all, she doesn't know this area. I should have made plans to make Sunday less lonely. I know she hates the quiet and the routine. So why didn't I deal with it?* She stopped in front of Kenny, whose eyes were tracking her back and forth. "Kenny, we have to find her."

He eased himself up. "You stay put. She might show up and it'd be good for you to be here. That way you can give her a whack on her backside while you're riled. I'll take the truck and drive into town."

She has to be safe, Kay thought. *And what if she isn't?* As Kenny drove down the driveway, she felt the sting of tears in her eyes. If Shawna was gone, the space she left behind would be bigger than Kay had ever imagined possible. In such a short time, and in spite of all the disruption . . . No. She couldn't say disruption, because that wasn't what Shawna's being there had become. Somehow, this brazen sixteen-year-old had shaken her awake and alive. She worried about her. Yet she somehow felt the stir of hope—for this girl and her future. Even that word had meaning again. "*Future*," she said, liking the sound in her ears.

Kay wiped her eyes with the back of her hand. If Kenny finds her, and if she comes back safe . . ."I'll make this work. I'll get her the help she needs. I'll do whatever it takes to save Nic's girl."

When Casey drove up for work, Kay made another turn around the house and then out to the barn, just in case Shawna had gone for a walk and returned.

"Did you see Shawna along the road when you came in?" she asked Casey.

"No, Ms. Stone. Sorry. Is anything wrong?"

She sighed. "I'm not sure. I think she's just escaped Sunday on the ranch, but she didn't tell me, so I'm a little worried."

He shook his head. "She doesn't make it easy for you, does she?"

"No."

"Must be Las Vegas manners." He turned to go into the barn. "If you need me to help, let me know, okay?"

She nodded. "Thank you, Casey."

As she walked up the back steps and into the kitchen, she heard the sound of the truck and ran to the front porch. Was Shawna in the passenger seat? Yes. Relief spread warm and clean through her. Then she got mad. What was she riding, a roller coaster? Fear. Relief. Anger. And a thousand pounds of doubt. She was up, down, around, and on her head. And all because of Shawna Stone, who sat next to Kenny Fargo, looking like she'd just come back from a vacation.

Chapter 28

Shawna

Nobody ever worried about where I went or when I came home. I was the one who worried. I was the one who bugged the guards to find Mom inside the casinos and the bars when she didn't show up at the apartment by 6:00 A.M. I took care of me and Mom when she crashed and burned. So what's the big deal about going into town without telling someone?

I get out of the truck. Kenny and Buster skirt the house and head straight for the barn.

Cowards.

In the living room, Kay paces in front of me, her hands waving all over the place, like she's talking to God. She isn't saying anything, but her body is shouting, and it's got a vocabulary that can singe your heart. When she stops, her eyes stare out from behind one of those tragic Greek masks.

"Do you know what it's like to wait for somebody to come home and not know where they are or what they are doing or if they've been hurt or what—?"

Do I! I'd like to tell her about some of those nights. Waiting for Mom. Wondering if she was coming back to the apartment or staying someplace else. And if she did come back, who or what she'd bring along. I shrug.

"Damn it!" She punches the air and bolts to the end of the living room.

My mouth drops. I've pissed her off, all right.

"Why do you do these things? Do you want to hurt me? Do you want to make my life as miserable as possible?"

"I didn't think going into town was going to make you miserable," I answer, and it's not a lie.

It's like someone opened a valve on a blow-up mattress and let all the air out. She collapses in the nearest chair and stares at the floor.

"I'm not used to being a grandmother. I don't even know what grandmothers are supposed to do these days. Mine baked birthday cakes for me and told me bedtime stories." She covers her face with both her hands and mumbles through her fingers. "You're too old for bedtime stories."

"Wow, cakes," I say, but I didn't mean it in a bad way. I never thought about someone baking me a birthday cake.

She stares at the floor. Then in a voice that sounds like she's reining it in tight, she says: "Shawna, we have an appointment with a therapist next Wednesday afternoon, after school. We are going in there and we are going to find out what each of us has to do to get along together. I don't care what you tell her or how you feel about going. I only care that each of us survives and maybe comes out somewhat whole at the end."

She stands up and gives me that red-eyed look of hers. "I'll pick you up exactly at 3 o'clock after school." She disappears down the hall and she doesn't exactly slam her office door, but it closes harder than usual.

I never got mad when Mom snuck out late and hit the tables. I never yelled at her about being the responsible person and letting me know where she was going and when she was leaving. I never . . . And what if I had? What difference would that have made? I make a circle with my thumb and first finger and hold it up. "Zero. Zip. Nada."

So what's with The Queen? Why's she so sensitive? Manual Entry #5: Keep Her Informed About Where You Go. Ha, like there are so many choices.

I pound the cushion next to me and push my face into it. Lights dance behind my eyelids, and I lie there, trying to digest what Kay said. I think about what happened in the café with Casey and then with that creep, and why the visit to The Troll's house weirded me out so much. "I don't know how many more Sundays I can do here," I whisper into the cushion.

I stretch up from the sofa and walk outside. There's still a lot of the day left, and no prospects of anything happening until dinner. *Whoopie!*

I think about taking Magic an apple and talking to him. Then I think about never seeing him again, and my throat burns like it did when Casey told me about Texas and what it means for horses. *I hate this place! I wish I'd never come here.*

I walk to the end of the house and look across at Drunk Floyd's. Magic hangs his long neck over the top rail and rubs against the rough wood. The other two lean against the shady side of the barn and twitch their tails. *Why's that dumb horse standing there in the hot sun? I know why.*

"Stupid animal!" But I'm already walking into the kitchen. I grab an apple and cut it up the way he likes it. I stashed the vitamins from Rural Supply at the back of the cabinet under the sink, so I grab the now very legal bottle, shake out two pills, and hurry down the back steps.

I climb up and over the fence and Magic has already taken a chunk of apple before I land. I grind the pills and stir them in a pan of water. He cleans the pan then nudges me until I rub the white spot on his head, something that pleases him now that he's used to me.

"Come on, let's get out of the sun. Don't you think it's hot enough to cook your hide out here?"

He follows me under the shade tree, eats the rest of his apple, and keeps nosing me for more. "That's it. I'll bring you another one tomorrow. Maybe." He rubs against my side, the hair on my arms tingles under his hot breath. I bite my lip hard.

I check the water trough and make sure all three horses have grass hay, but Magic, ignoring the fresh hay, trails after me as I make my way back to Kay's.

"What's up with you today?" I reach my arms up around his neck.

Stay, he says to me, or at least I think that's what he'd say if he could. *Ride with me.*

This is great, now I'm starting the Sweet River mind

reading, only I'm reading what's going on inside a horse's head? "I . . . I . . . don't know how, Magic."

I'll teach you. Climb on that fence and put your leg over my back. I'll teach you to ride. I'll teach you to do a lot of things, Shawna. Try. Don't be afraid.

"I'm not afraid of anything. Why is everybody and everything on the planet trying to tag me with that?"

Magic snorts and paws the ground. Now he's giving me that stare. That, "You-Can't-Kid-Me, Kid," look that The Queen uses.

"Okay." I glance away. "I'm afraid. You satisfied?"

He shakes his head.

"And if you tell another soul what I just said, I'll punch your lights out, buddy! Besides, you're not really so smart. If you were so smart, you wouldn't belong to Floyd now, would you?"

He butts me in my side with his head.

Don't be afraid.

He turns, walks to the fence, and waits for me to catch up.

The best way to do anything that's new, and not too much to your liking, is to do it fast. But Magic is suddenly ten stories taller than he was a minute ago, and his back looks slick as oil. I'm going to fall and break bones. I just know it.

He gives me another look. *Well?*

"If I die, you are gonna hear from my lawyers."

Funny. I said, if.

I climb to the top rail, balance; then swing my leg over Magic's back before I give another thought to the prospects of not getting down again in one piece.

He stands until I have a grip on his mane, and then he takes me with him. I cinch my thighs tight against his sides, squeeze my eyes shut, and wonder what in the hell I think I'm doing on the back of this humongous animal. I relax my grip and he picks up his pace. Now he is sort of jogging, or whatever horses do, and my butt is slapping against his back.

"I'm not good at this, Magic. Slow down, okay?"

You'll get better. Riding is easy. It's like breathing.

"Right. And I don't do that so good, either. Maybe I need breathing lessons before I take your riding lessons."

He shifts into another gear, and now I feel like I'm on a ship, rocking forward and back. I squeeze my legs tighter and lean over his broad neck.

He slows, and I'm back to the butt-slapping again, until he drops to a walk and returns me to the fence.

Now you can climb down. You're free to go.

I climb onto the fence and watch Magic walk to the barn.

"I'll bring you an apple tomorrow after school!" I yell.

He doesn't look back at me.

"If you're still alive," I say. I kick the fence post hard. "Ow!" Hopping and holding onto the toe of my tennis shoe I ask myself, *When . . . did you . . . decide to . . . ow . . . be stupid?* I sit and pull my shoe off. My sock is bloody. *You're such a loser. And you can't help it, can you?*

As carefully as I can, I peel the sock off. My big toe kinda waggles when I touch it. The nail is bleeding, and a dark bruise already covers it all the way to the joint.

"It's broken." Casey is looking down at me.

"Oh, no." I drop my bloody sock and cover my face with my hands. *Maybe if I block out all the light, I'll be safe. I don't want him here. I don't need him here. I don't want or need anybody or anything. But damn, I wish my toe would stop throbbing.*

I feel his arms reach under and lift me. I keep my face covered so I don't have to see him, so I can't see where he's taking me. I can feel his chest rising and falling, his heartbeat against my side. I'm thinking about those movies, with strong men sweeping up sexy women and . . . and my toe is ready to explode. Why doesn't he say something? If he says anything, I'll pop him in the nose. My toe has a heart of its own now, and that heart is drumming so hard my whole foot throbs.

"What's this, something we have to shoot and put out of her misery?"

I peek through my fingers at Kenny Fargo, who sits rocking in his favorite chair on the front porch.

"Broken toe is all," Casey says. He puts me on the step and walks away. "Shoot her if that's what you need to do."

"Looks like you got yourself another friend," Kenny said, nodding toward Casey's retreating back.

Chapter 29

Kay

Monday morning Kay dropped Shawna at school. "Shawna, are you sure you can walk on that foot today?"

"It's fine."

"All right, but call me if you have problems later." Kay waited until Shawna limped inside the front door with her books hugged to her chest.

After a few errands, she returned home and was putting groceries away when the phone rang. Kay answered, expecting a call from the vet.

"Kay, it's Jackie."

The flat, nasal voice Kay would never forget jolted her as sharply as an electrical charge. Pictures from over sixteen years ago flashed in her head like a slide show. Nicholas, sitting with his elbows on the kitchen table, his hands covering his face. Jackie, standing next to him. Peter, standing near the back door, looking out. *Where was she?* Behind the camera, she guessed, because she couldn't see herself. It was probably better that she didn't.

Kay gripped the phone tighter. "What do you want?"

She didn't waste intonation on the question, so her voice sounded as flat as the one on the other end of the line.

"I'd like to talk to Shawna."

"She's in school."

"When—"

"She'll be home after three."

"I'll call back then."

Kay hung up the phone.

The next call came before Kay's hand left the receiver, and this time it was the vet. She made arrangements with him to come to the barn later and check on the gray. The rest of the day, she went from worrying over the gray's condition to trying her best not to think about Jackie. But even while Kay sat watching over her horse, Jackie was never out of her mind.

She walked between the barn and the house, talking to herself. "The last thing I need is that one back in my life. What are you talking about, Kay? She'll always be in your life, as long as Shawna's around."

At 2:30, Kay climbed into the truck. Buster jumped into the bed and they were on their way to pick up Shawna. It was a routine now, one she and Buster had built into their weekdays. It gave Kay time to think about her day, to worry over the gray's temperature that Kenny couldn't get down to normal, to remind herself to make Kenny's apple pie as she'd promised, to put together a mental list of errands she still needed to do before dinner. The ten-minute ride was Kay's break.

She turned into the school parking lot and drove to the front. Shawna stood on the steps, her chin jutting out, her hip swished to one side, where she'd propped her books. When she looked up, her expression surprised Kay. It was the first time her granddaughter looked happy to see her. Something warm flooded the inside of her chest, and she had to grip the wheel to keep back the tears that threatened.

Shawna limped to the truck and climbed inside.

"How's the toe?"

"Whaddya think? It still hurts."

The same smart sass came out of Shawna's mouth when she answered, and Kay's fuzzy feeling evaporated. She pointed to the seat belt. Next she'd get a recording and play "Buckle up" every time the girl got in. She may be an AP student, Kay thought, but she doesn't remember anything she's told.

She should warn the girl about Jackie's call, but maybe Jackie'd forget to call back. Reliable was not an adjective that woman could even spell.

As they drove up to the house, Kenny came out to meet them and gave Shawna a hand up the front steps. For a moment Kay thought about the ranch without Shawna, but she pushed that thought aside and opened the door for the doctor and his patient.

"Go into Kay's office," Kenny told Shawna. "I'll get my bag."

Kenny's bag was a magical leather pouch that held dozens of ointments, pills, and bandages. No matter how many things he retrieved from inside it, he could always extract something more. Even the vet borrowed from Kenny's bag. Kay once asked him how he knew so much about medicine. But she never did again, because his face had shifted into such despair that she instantly regretted her question. How he learned the art of healing didn't matter anyway.

"I'll leave you to your doctoring. I'm going out to see if the gray looks any better after a few hours on this new antibiotic." Kay walked to the barn and opened the gray's stall.

"How's it going, girl?" Kay took the gray's head in her lap and gently rubbed the broad forehead. The gray turned her eyes to meet Kay's. Kay was the love of her life. The person she trusted above all. It was all there in those dark windows that allowed Kay a glimpse into her cherished horse.

The vet was coming again tomorrow. Kenny said he'd sleep in the barn tonight. She had nothing to worry about, yet she couldn't hold down the bile that crept into her throat when she thought about the possibility that the gray might not recover.

"You have to make it, girl. I need you. I need you desperately." Kay buried her face in the great neck.

Too many feelings swirled inside her. Jackie's phone call had brought back the day Nicholas told them he was not going to college. He couldn't. Jackie needed him. There was a baby on the way.

"If it's too late for an abortion, put the baby up for adoption. We'll help you. We'll take care of the bills, the arrangements, anything. But please, Nic, go to college!" She heard her words over and over. She watched Nicholas take Jackie's hand, lead her past his father, and out the back door to his car. She never saw either of them again.

The gray tossed her head. "Okay, girl. You rest. I'll be back to check on you."

Kenny passed her on his way to his trailer. "Missy will live," he said. "How's the mare?"

"No change."

Kenny nodded and walked on. After a few steps he called to her. "Call came."

Kay waved over her shoulder without looking back at him. She went inside and down the hall to her office, where she leaned against the door, watching Shawna, who sat staring at the receiver in her hand.

"I see you got your call. She phoned earlier and I told her you'd be here about this time." Kay walked to the desk. "How's the toe?"

She wanted to talk about something else, yet she needed to know what Jackie wanted. She sat on the couch, trying to look interested rather than anxious. "So what does she want?"

She knew the answer before Shawna said a word. Back to Las Vegas and that hell Jackie called a life. *No!* She wanted to scream. *You can't go back. You belong here.*

"She sounded . . . lonely, I guess," Shawna said. An expression of longing flitted across her face.

An emotion other than anger, Kay thought with surprise. Maybe I'm wrong in trying to keep her here. Maybe she should be with her mother.

"Yes, I imagine she did." Kay couldn't stay in the room another minute. "I'll go and start dinner." She ran out the back door and hid in the barn with the gray until she'd cried it out, feeling somewhat better prepared to fry chicken without self-destructing in the process.

Chapter 30

Shawna

I hate Sundays like I hate big snakes with fangs. I hate Mondays like any kind of snake, so what's to choose? Today's not going to be easy. My foot feels like it's in a bucket.

When Kay drops me off at the front entrance, she looks worried. "Shawna are you sure you can walk on that foot today?"

"It's fine." I'm lying, but I don't want to stay on the ranch, watching the minute hands on the kitchen clock all day. I limp up the steps and go inside.

Casey is coming down the hall, so I duck into the girls' restroom. No way am I letting him see me, now that I'm old limp-along. When I'm sure Casey's gone, I make my way to class. There I get lots of stares but no sympathy, except from Mrs. Heady, and I can do without hers.

The Troll, aka Marta, smiles when I make it to my seat at the back of the room. I don't snarl at her, but I don't smile back, either. At least she doesn't smell today. Maybe she got the hint about the high correlation between her B.O. and her lack of popularity with me.

I can do Mrs. Heady's assignment without breaking a sweat, so I finish in a flash and bury my head under my arms. Naps help Mondays go faster.

"Psst!"

What sounds like a leaky gas pipe turns out to be Marta.

I roll my head to the side and glare at her.

"Here, take this," she whispers.

She's holding a folded piece of paper out to me across the aisle.

I sigh and snatch it from her hand. What's she up to now? Please tell me she doesn't want to bond.

The note reads, "My mom says I can have a sleepover next weekend. Can you come?"

Oh, gawd! It's an invitation to sleep with The Troll. Now what? I know Mondays are the worst, but this is the grimmest in history. Just bring on the snakes and get it over with.

"I'll think about it," I whisper. And I'm not sure I'm hearing myself correctly. *What's to think about?*

When school's over, it's a major relief to see Kay's beat up old truck pull to a stop in front of the school. Buster's in back, yapping and shaking himself like a berserk windup toy. I double-quick-hobble to the curb and hoist myself inside.

"How's the toe?" Kay asks.

"Whaddya think? It still hurts."

"We'll check it when we get home. Toes mend fast, especially when Kenny tends to them." She points at the seat belt.

Right.

We jostle home, and I mark off another day at Sweet River High. *How many hundreds are left, anyway? Who knows?*

As "Dr. Fargo" kneels to unwind the bandage around my big toe, I grip the chair in Kay's office, which doubles as our family clinic. But he doesn't hurt me, and when I look, the swelling is down and the toe looks pretty much the same shape as it did before I Karate-kicked the fence post.

"Looks like we won't have to amputate." Kenny smiles up at me. "Stick your foot in this tub and keep it there for ten minutes. I'll be back."

So now I'm stuck behind Kay's command central desk, with my foot in a tub of water. Does life get any better?

The sharp sound of the phone on Kay's desk sends a lightning jolt right through me. I lift the receiver. "Hello."

"Shawna. It's me . . . Mom." Her voice fills my right ear, and I instantly get the shakes.

She actually called herself Mom. That means she's alone.

"How are you, Honey? . . . Shawna? . . . You there, Baby?"

"I'm here."

"Well, look. I'm back in Vegas. That thing with Dylan didn't work out." She clears her throat. "I'm really missing you, Sweetie. I need you to come on back. I really mean that. We can find a place together and it'll be like old times!"

157

I pull the phone away from my ear and stare at it. I wonder how she'd look if she were really tucked inside that plastic case, wound in and out of all the pieces connecting sound between Las Vegas and Sweet River.

"Shawna? What the hell is wrong with you? Why are you taking, like, forever to answer me?"

"I'm thinking, Mom."

Her sigh travels the miles, down the dark Vegas alleys, across the flat desert, winding up through the center of California, where it washes over me.

I lay my cheek on Kay's desk and feel the cool wood against it. I'll disappear inside the dark thick-grained surface, where nobody will ever find me. But I'll stare up at the ceiling, feeling the pressure of Kay's hands, as she writes letters and leans on me for balance. I'll see the world from a safe place, from a place that's only for me.

"Fuck, Shawna. How come you have to give something like this so much thought? You and me make a team, right?"

"What, are you broke?"

Now it's her end that goes quiet.

I can wait for her to come up with an answer. I've waited before, sometimes I've waited all night, for more important reasons than a yes or a no.

☙

That night she brought Dylan home the first time, that was a hundred years of waiting. I was zonked out, nested

158

inside my sheets on Tuan's roll-away bed, when a voice whispered in my ear. "Hey, come on, Baby, your big sister's passed out and I'm lonely."

My big sister? I'm dreaming, right? So I rolled over and punched my pillow. That's when his wormy fingers slid under my belly and down my leg.

"What in the . . .!" I was up and standing before he could get off his knees by the bed. "I gotta pee. I'll be right back."

He sprawled across my roll-way and I staggered to the bathroom.

Click. Door locked.

I realized my mistake too late. No dry towels and only one skimpy bathmat. I pushed the mat into the corner and curled up with my legs tucked against my chest. Talk about misery! And my *big sister* didn't haul herself out of bed to pee until two o'clock in the morning.

U

"Look." Mom's phone voice cuts through the memory of that night on the bathroom floor. "Here's a number you can call me at. I'm around after noon and before ten. You know me, Shawna, that's still kinda my schedule." She makes a noise that passes for a laugh. "Got a pencil?"

"Yes." I pick up a pencil and write the number.

"Okay, hon, I gotta go. You call me, okay? Shawna?"

"I'll call you."

The phone hums. She's gone.

"I see you got your call." Kay is standing in the door-way. "She phoned earlier and I told her you'd be here about this time." She walks to the desk. "How's the toe?"

"Kenny says I can keep it on the foot."

"That Kenny! Makes things light, doesn't he?" Kay sits on the couch opposite the desk. "So what does she want?"

I'll bet Kay knows the answer to that question already. She's mining for information just like that princi-pal. They're like a pair of cops. Well, give the answer anyway. Play her game. "She wants me to go back to Vegas. Her boyfriend is out of the picture."

"I see."

I see? Look at Kay's face. She doesn't see anything. "She sounded . . . lonely, I guess."

"Yes. I imagine she did." Kay stands. "I'll go and start dinner."

And she's gone, just like that! She can't wait to pack me into the truck and drive me back to the bus station. Good. Fine. Great. The sooner I'm out of here, the better. I can forget all this Sweet River crap and get back to where I belong.

Chapter 31

Kay

Wednesday, and the appointment with the therapist, at first came too slowly, and then too soon. Kay stood at her closet, looking for something to wear—something not made of denim.

Would Shawna meet her on time in front of the school? Would she cooperate during the session? Would the session make a positive difference? In two hours, three people were coming together to sort out several things that terrified Kay. Life and death; Shawna and herself.

Kay chose the black suit from the two she still kept for the occasional funeral or wedding, or that rare trip to Sacramento when she needed to see a ballet. She unzipped the garment bag she'd hung it in a year ago. There weren't that many weddings anymore and, thank heaven, the funerals had tapered off as well. When she lost her enthusiasm for seeing the ballet alone, the black suits worked their way into the recesses of her closet.

She glanced at her watch: 2:15 P.M. She'd made the counseling appointment for 4:30 P.M., and Shawna had promised to meet her in front of the school at 3:00 P.M.

Beyond that, Shawna hadn't promised anything, especially cooperation.

Kay showered, dressed, and brushed her dark hair into a sleek mane at the nape of her neck, where she caught it in a burnished gold clasp. Gray strands threaded their way alongside her temples, but, like her mother's and grandmother's, her hair still looked like a forty-year-old's. She touched the skin under her eyes, which told a different story.

"Too much sun," she said to her image. "Grandmother warned you, but did you listen?" She quickly daubed creamy lotion from a sample jar that some chirpy clerk had thrust into her hand one day at Drugs For Less. "Maybe I should get more of this stuff."

"Are you ready?" Kenny called from outside.

She wriggled her feet into the black heels she'd set by the bed, and felt her toes pinch tight against each other. "Ugh." Her feet couldn't still be growing. She opened her bedroom door and replied, "Coming."

Kenny met her on the front porch. "My. My. My. We do look fine."

"So, do I look like I'm on the way to analysis?"

"Nope. But it don't matter how you look. It matters how you feel."

"Does *stressed* give you some idea?" Kay wanted to shove her hands into her pockets, but she didn't have any.

"You got a filly that needs help, and you're giving her the only help you know how. Too bad she ain't truly a horse. Then we'd both know what to do, no question."

"Right." Kay heaved a sigh. "So you washed the truck, I see."

Kenny had driven the truck up to the front of the house, trailing drips of water down the driveway. It didn't shine, but the dust was gone and the windshield glinted in the late afternoon sun.

"It'll get you there and back. It's got gas and the keys are in it." Kenny walked down the steps then stopped and looked at her. "Try smiling when you pick her up. You're not taking her to her hanging, you know."

No. Not to hers, Kay thought, *but maybe to mine*, as she walked to the truck and climbed in.

Shawna kept her promise. She was waiting on the curb when Kay drove up. She climbed in and pulled the door closed. "Wow! Who did the number on Mr. Bumpy here?"

Kay's sour answer was out of her mouth before she could stop it. She wished that just once she could say what she wanted to say. Exactly who was pushing whom away in this relationship? "Kenny did his best to make it look good." She attempted to sound positive, but the words came out flat.

That was as close to opening a conversation as she could manage. Then Shawna said nothing more, and Kay was too nervous to think about anything except the appointment they were about to keep.

"Seat belt."

The trip to Sacramento seemed to take hours. Kay worried that she'd never make it on time, even though she was traveling against the commuter traffic. Why did everyone in California suddenly decide this hot-as-hell-in-the-summer place was the only one to live in? Every time she drove this freeway, more earth disappeared and more mini-malls sprang up.

She took the T-Street turnoff and followed the directions from the therapist's secretary. After a few quick turns, she pulled into the underground parking with her heart racing.

She stepped from the truck, followed the arrows to the elevator, and pressed the button. Her hand shook.

"You okay?" Shawna asked.

"No. I'm not." How could she be okay? How could anybody be okay when they were about to meet a stranger, tell her all their secrets, and reveal the failure behind the bad decisions made over a lifetime.

Stop, Kay. You're not revealing anything. You're offering up your last child in the hopes that you can undo a few of those bad decisions while there's still time.

They stepped into the elevator, and it took them to the sixth floor without the stop that Kay kept hoping for. Delay was on her mind, postponement in her heart.

But the receptionist had other ideas. "Dr. Lubell asked that you come right in." She led them to a double oak door, knocked, and ushered them inside. "Mrs. Stone and Shawna Stone," she said, before closing the door softly behind her.

Chapter 32

Shawna

By Wednesday, Casey is avoiding me as much as I'm avoiding him. Good.

He's coming down the hall now. I stare straight ahead, walking directly toward my locker. As we pass, he's talking with somebody, too busy to look in my direction. Good again. I'm still lame, so I don't need him laughing at me, the idiot who kicks posts. I don't need any more of his preachy, "tucked-under-my heart" crap. Besides, I've got to think over how I'm going to handle that appointment with the shrink.

I should have rehearsed in front of the mirror to get my face to match my answers. *My grandmother is a wonderful woman. I'm just a little upset about my mom, but I'm managing, coping, recovering. Hmm. Maybe adjusting. That's a good shrink word. I really don't know why Mr. Green thinks I have a problem. I'm getting used to . . . adjusted . . . to a very different way of living, you know?*

"Hi, Shawna!"

Arrrg. Marta is right behind me.

"Did you ask your grandmother about the sleepover?"

"Umm, not yet." I twirl my lock and pop the door open.

"You're not even thinking about asking her, right?"

"What's with you? Why do you think you can read my mind?" I slam my locker and face her. "What time should I be there?"

"You're coming?"

"Not unless you tell me when to show up. I don't read minds like you do."

"It's Saturday at seven. Mom's getting us something to eat, like pizza, I guess. So far, there're just four of us."

I hadn't thought about the possibility that other girls would be at her house. I'm not sure I can handle two more girls in that one room of hers. Besides, I don't like sleeping in front of people I don't know. "Who else?"

"You met them once, but you don't really know them. I don't think you do, anyway." Marta laughs. "See, I can't read minds. Anyway, they want to know what Las Vegas is like. What you're like."

Marta chatters on and on, and I'm like, thinking, *What the hell. I'm out of here soon anyway, so why not? This is probably gonna be the first and last sleepover of my life, so it doesn't really matter.* "I'll ask Kay to drive me to town. I'll come if she'll bring me."

"That's super!"

Suddenly Marta is a grateful golden retriever. What have I done?

"I've got class," I say. "Gotta go." But I'm not getting away. She's in lock step with me down the hall to Chemistry. I've got a buddy, a pal. Just what I've always wanted. Sit. Stay. Roll over.

I promised to meet Kay at the curb at exactly three o'clock, so when Chemistry class ends, I'm doing my best to be on time, but Marta's not helping me get out of there.

"My mom's letting us have the whole place to ourselves. She's really excited you're coming too because . . . well, she's just excited. Bring your sleeping bag, and if you've got CDs, I just got this really cool—"

"Okay, Marta. I got the idea. I'll be there. But I gotta go meet Kay right now."

Finally she gets the message and I drag myself out the door and down the steps with two minutes to spare.

When the truck rattles to a stop in front of me, I glance at my watch. Three o'clock. I shake my head. How can she always be exactly on time?

I climb in. I want to whistle because she looks totally cool. Instead I look at the truck and say, "Wow! Who did the number on Mr. Bumpy here?" Kay looks so grim that I think a little humor might make the trip easier.

But she doesn't smile. "It wasn't me." She looks at me and I get the feeling she wants to start over from when I first got in the truck. "Kenny washed it," she says with what sounds like a sigh. "Seat belt."

Once. Just once, I wish she'd forget the friggin' seat belt.

It's the usual silent running. Kay should have been a submarine captain. But I can tell from the way she grips the steering wheel that she's a total wreck. *Hey*, I want to say. *It's my head they're examining, so what're you all twisted about?*

We pull into the parking garage, and without waiting for me to close the truck door, she's loping off across the garage to the elevator. What's with her, anyway?

"You okay?" I ask, knowing from the way her hand's shaking, that she's not.

"No. I'm not," she snaps.

"I didn't think so."

I think, *Then why in hell did you do this? I don't need a shrink. I don't want a shrink. I may get down sometimes, but who doesn't? Even horses, right?*

And now I'm thinking about Magic. How he talks to me. How he knows me better than any shrink ever could. He even knows me better than that creep, Monster. *Easy, girl. You want the shrink to hear you talking with Magic or Monster? Let those items slip, and you'll be in a padded cell seeing major shrinks every day.*

In the elevator, Kay's eyes are closed. Is she praying? We stop at the sixth floor. Kay heaves one shaky sigh, then she's out the door.

Okay, Ms. Shrink. Here come Shawna and The Stone.

Chapter 33

Kay

When the receptionist announced them and shut the door, Dr. Lubell rose from behind her desk and held out her hand. "Welcome. Please sit down."

Kay took a seat on the couch as the therapist indicated. Her armpits felt damp, just the way they did that first day when Shawna arrived at the bus depot. Kay wanted in the worst way to lift her hair up from the back of her neck. If she hadn't known better, she'd have sworn her hot flashes had returned.

"Do you want to begin by talking about what brought you here to see me?" Dr. Lubell asked.

What has brought me here? Kay suddenly wondered. *Was it really Shawna's problems, or were they mine that did it? Family issues. What were they?* Her well-organized spreadsheet of causes and effects had scattered like autumn leaves. She didn't know how to answer the doctor's question.

Kay leaned forward and put her arms across her knees before she realized that this was how she sat when she had serious business to discuss with Kenny. She missed the feel of her jeans against her legs. She missed the comfort of her old friend listening to her problems.

Finally she spoke: "I'm worried about my grand-daughter." She sat back against the hard sofa cushion and took a moment to think about what she needed to say to this woman who was sitting across from her. *Make it simple*, she thought.

She wished the therapist wore glasses, didn't have perfect, white-tipped fingernails, didn't look like she was just out of college. Kay couldn't shake the feeling that she was at a social gathering, about to reveal private secrets to a gossip columnist.

Suddenly her throat went dry, and no amount of swallowing helped. The words in her head came to her lips, and she watched as Dr. Lubell nodded her very blond head. Kay prayed that what she was saying made sense.

"I'm not . . ." Kay thought that maybe, if she cleared her throat, her reason for being here would be easier to express. ". . . handling the situation well." She heard her own words, but they seemed to come from someone else's lips. ". . . I just don't know how." She heard herself utter that sentence, because that was the most important part of the whole speech. It was painfully true, too, and it exhausted her to say it. She was glad for the leather sofa at her back.

It was Dr. Lubell's turn. "Shawna, do you want to say anything about your grandmother's concern?"

Shawna glared at first the doctor, then at Kay. Kay felt the heat of Shawna's anger, along with her own rising tide of self-doubt. Had she been right in demanding to sit in on this first session despite the doctor's wish to meet with Shawna alone?

But she couldn't just leave Shawna stranded with someone neither of them knew. Kay was nervous enough herself. How would Shawna feel, especially alone in this room with a stranger, even if she was a doctor? Kay rubbed her eyes. Robby had asked for the same privacy, and he'd talked her out of staying. And she regretted not being there in that room, being with Shawna while Robby asked her his questions. Was she making mistake after mistake?

Shawna scowled at Kay and shoved the neat pile of magazines across the glass table. "What's all this crap about me being angry?"

She is angry, Kay wanted to scream. *Why else would she act the way she does? Why else would she look at me with eyes that shoot bullets?*

Dr. Lubell was saying something about anger . . . about being pissed. My god, she sounded like Shawna.

Shawna let loose with her mouth from hell and shouted back at the doctor.

It was the therapist's turn, "Do you want to talk about why you're pissed?"

As Shawna jumped up from the couch, Kay felt as though someone had drained any energy she had in reserve, quickly pouring it onto the carpet. She looked up at her granddaughter, thinking that yelling never calms a horse. So she quietly said, "Shawna, sit down, please."

After Shawna's outburst, the room became silent, as if it were pulling back just like its occupants, and regrouping for the next verbal onslaught. Kay just kept still and listened.

Dr. Lubell then asked Shawna, "Is there anything you feel comfortable sharing about yourself?"

Kay squeezed her fists so hard, her nails nearly cut into her palms.

Shawna shook her head. Then, in that way she had of becoming absent, disappeared inside her skin. Her eyes roved the room desperately.

Escape? Is that what she's looking for? Kay wondered.

"Do you have any idea why your principal might think you're depressed? Why he suggested you talk to me?" Dr. Lubell asked softly.

Tell her about the picture, Shawna. Tell her what you wrote, how you reject everyone. Tell her!

But Shawna did exactly what Kay expected. She shrugged.

"Do you know what I mean when I use the word *depressed?*"

"No."

Maybe I shouldn't have brought her here. Maybe the school's way off base. I need some kind of grandmother's manual, because I know I'm doing everything wrong. Pay attention, Kay. Pay attention. I'm trying.

"I like ice cream."

What? What did she say about ice cream?

"Me too," Dr. Lubell said.

And Shawna's smiling? What did I miss? Pay attention.

"What do you want different in your life?" Dr. Lubell asked, and Kay held her breath for the answer. She had so many things she wanted to say. *I want my granddaughter to love me. I want to love her. I want my son back. I want my life back the way it should be.* But the question wasn't hers to answer, so she waited for what Shawna would say.

Shawna, the smile gone so quickly that Kay doubted she'd seen it at all, sat with her eyes closed. Her jaw was set in that way she held it when she wanted to explode, when the full force of her anger ran free.

Yes, Kay thought, *she holds back a lot of what's inside her. . . everything except language that could singe a hide from twenty feet. That, she never holds back.*

Kay was tired and hot. She wanted to rip off her suit and free her feet from their misery. She wanted to get out of this office. So far, Dr. Lubell hadn't done more than ask a few questions. Was this all there was to counseling? What had she expected? A miracle, that's what.

Shawna opened her eyes at last. "I want . . . to go home," she said.

Home? Did she say, home? Kay leaned her head back against the couch. Suddenly it was too heavy to hold up.

Chapter 34

Shawna

When the receptionist introduces us, I'm thinking, *Who in the hell is Shawna Stone?*

You, dummy.

Me?

Yes. That's your real name.

Is that the name I'll keep forever?

Why not? Here lies Shawna Stone, chiseled in . . . you guessed it, Stone!

Does having a real name make me more real?

I think this is a question for the shrink, who isn't what I expected. I pictured her with thick specs and bangs, but even as old as she must be, she still qualifies as hot.

And I'm still trying to digest seeing my grandmother in a black silk suit that curves over her hips. She looks pretty sharp in her white silk shirt, with no plaid anywhere in sight. A tiny gold chain gleams at her throat, and she's wearing black leather heels, which shoot her another two inches up into the stratosphere.

Kay sits sweating on the couch, like she's just crossed

the finish line. It's time to play their game, so I sit next to her and try on my obedient face.

The therapist sits opposite us on another couch. Between us is a glass coffee-table with a stack of magazines and a small silver bowl. The room around us glows with light, but I don't see a single lamp.

The shrink leans back and folds her hands in her lap like she's settling in for the long haul. "Do you want to begin by talking about what's brought you in to see me?" She looks at me and then at Kay. I have an answer to her question, but I'm not answering questions today. You want to hear what I'd tell Ms. Shrink if I was in the mood? I'd say, a truck. A beat up, hammered piece of shit. That's what brought me here.

"I only spoke with you on the phone briefly, Mrs. Stone. But you seemed to feel it would be helpful for you and Shawna if you could both talk to someone to work through some family issues."

What family issues? Maybe I need to ask questions instead of answer them.

My grandmother leans forward and puts her arms on her knees. "I'm worried about my granddaughter. Shawna is—" She stares at the tabletop then sits back again, like she's rehearsing her words inside her head. "Her principal and her teacher think she needs to talk to a professional who knows how to work with a young person who . . . who might be . . . depressed."

Kay swallows hard and her gold chain shines in the magic light. "I get the feeling she's angry at me . . . at everything and everybody. When she's not angry, she doesn't seem to care about anything."

I'm listening to her like she's talking about somebody I don't know. It's interesting to hear her describe somebody, and how they act and what they feel. She's talking about Shawna Stone. *Don't know her. Sorry.*

"I'm not," Kay clears her throat, "handling the situation well. I just don't know how." Kay sits back now, as though she's used up her batteries and needs to recharge.

The shrink nods. "Shawna, do you want to say anything about your grandmother's concern?"

I shake my head.

"She said you seem angry at her, and she'd like to understand what she can do to perhaps work through that anger with you."

I close my eyes. I hate being here, and I shove the stack of magazines across the table. They hit the silver bowl and it clatters to the center.

"What's all this crap about me being angry?"

"I can see I've pissed you off. But I'd really like to know you, so I don't want to do that again."

I can't read her face. I can't tell where she's going with all this blah blah. I don't say another word.

"I see that you don't want to talk about how you're feeling." She cocks her head at me, and I stare back. "That's okay. Maybe another time."

Who's the nut here? Why would I talk to her about anything? I'm being drilled by a psycho-shrink hottie, and corralled by granny-in-a-suit next to me. I'd like to walk out right now, just slam the door in their faces. I didn't expect this party with mood lighting. I've got other things to do with my time.

Kay's gone mute and practically buried herself into

the leather couch. I wonder if she'll sink inside and disappear. The hottie is looking at me, her expression as flat as if she's ironed it on.

It's so quiet I can hear myself breathing. *How did I let Kay drag me here? Why? How can I get out of here, ASAP?*

"Okay, I'm pissed." She used that word so . . . I . . . CAN . . .TOO. I glare at my grandmother.

"Do you want to talk about why you're pissed?"

"I hate . . . your crappy questions . . . your—" I wave my arms "—crappy room. I feel like hurling this damned silver bowl against the wall and getting the hell out of here."

"I can understand your wanting to be someplace besides this stuffy office." She looks around her. "But are you willing to help out your grandmother and me by giving us a little time here?"

Huh?

"How about telling me where you'd like to be instead? Where do you like spending your time?"

I shoot up to my feet. "What you're asking, it's nobody's business."

"You're right, but I just want to know you better. Forget I asked you that question."

"Shawna, sit down, please," Kay says this softly, like she's too tired to raise her voice.

I melt into the chair. Suddenly I'm tired, too. I feel like I could sleep for a week.

"Let's start again, shall we?" The shrink's looking at me, waiting.

I'm not going to talk to her anymore.

"Is there anything you feel comfortable sharing about yourself? Something that will help your grandmother know what she can do to make things better between you?"

Now Kay is looking at me, too. I've got four eyes boring holes in me.

I shake my head and study the panels with their mystery light. Not one more word. No. I feel Monster's nudge, and the shaky feeling travels down into my stomach. I'd put my head on my lap if I were alone—if these two women weren't at me with all this drool. I don't want anybody to know me. And if I needed help, I'd ask for it. I don't need anything from anybody. Leave me alone. I do fine by myself, alone. Me and Mom . . . we do just fine alone. It goes south when other people mess with us . . . or with her. I push my hands under my thighs and wait for Monster to scram.

"Do you have any idea why your principal might think you're depressed?"

Hottie isn't letting up. I shrug.

Kay rubs her eyes.

"Do you know what I mean when I use that word *depressed?* It's used so much that I wonder if anyone really knows what it means anymore."

"No." That slips out before I catch myself.

"Would you like to find out?"

Would I? Hell, no. De = down, Pressed = pushed flat. That's enough.

For a while the shrink watches me, then asks, "What makes you happy, Shawna?"

Happy. That's the word Principal Green used. What is it about these people in California, always going on about being happy? They don't get it, do they? Happy isn't something I know much about. And even if it comes, it doesn't stay. Then that moment slips into my mind.

In a place I don't remember, the woman's long red braid is tied at the end with a velvet ribbon, and lying over her shoulder like a thick red rope.

I'm five. Mom is gone. The woman knocks at the door and asks why I'm crying. Then she props me up on pillows and feeds me ice cream, and I lick the spoon and she laughs and I laugh—

U

"I like ice cream," I say.

The shrink smiles. "Me, too."

I've said something right?

"If someone asked you what you wanted to change in your life, would you feel like answering that?" the shrink asks.

And while I've squeezed my eyes shut against the light, I'm wondering who in the hell wrote her script?

I don't want anything to be different in my life because there's no way anything else will be any better than what's happening right now.

But she's the first person who ever asked ME what I want. Me, Shawna Stone, or whoever the hell I am. Mom

179

never asks me what I want. She's always telling me what SHE wants . . . needs . . . has to have, or SHE'LL just die!

Kay never says anything, one way or the other, except for me to follow her rules. Any day she'll hook me to a lead and trot me around in a circle until I learn the steps as good as her gray does.

What *do* I want? *Give her something, Shawna. Anything.* And then go over that question later, when you're not being squeezed—de + pressed—for an answer.

I open my eyes and look straight at her. "I want . . . to go home." When I hear myself say the word, *home,* I don't believe what flashes in my brain. I don't see the Casino Royale, with all its lights and its racket. No. It's that damn red house with the barn, and Kenny Fargo hurling spit on the porch, with Kay leading the gray out to the trail, and me holding a stupid apple, my leg over the fence reaching out to Magic.

The shrink gives me that smile again. "Okay. We're done for today. I agreed to start by meeting with you and your grandmother together, briefly. Next time we'll talk longer, and it'll just be you and me." She stands. "Now, Shawna, go on home. It's a nice place to think over what we've talked about today, right?"

What just happened here? Did she just trap me? Did she make me say what she wanted me to say?

She has that look—the one a card counter at the blackjack table gets when he knows what the dealer's about to lay down.

I can't meet her eyes right now.

Chapter 35

Kay

"Shawna, I don't want to hear anymore!" Kay's head had been pounding since she'd left for the appointment with the therapist. During the session, she'd felt a vise tighten around her skull, and the fight with Shawna on the way home only made the pain worse. She gripped the wheel tight and willed herself not to throw up. She'd never had a migraine in her life, but she'd never had a possibly suicidal granddaughter before either.

Being jostled by the truck wasn't helping. She rubbed her eyes and decided she might have to consider buying one that actually had springs and didn't look like it had been through a demolition derby.

She turned off the main road onto what she referred to as her *arroyo seco—her dry brook*. More like a bucking bronco ride to hell.

"Oh, no!" The lights in the barn might as well have been a shrieking emergency alarm. The truck bounced down the road and up to the front of the house. She jumped out almost before the truck stopped moving, leaving the door sagging open on its hinges. She kicked off her heels and sprinted barefoot toward the barn.

When she reached the gray's stall, she entered a nightmare—a tableau of Kenny, the vet, and her beauty, her sleeping beauty. But no prince could wake her gray.

The men didn't speak as she knelt at the gray's side and stroked her neck. *Come back*, she thought. She looked at the gray's chest and hoped, praying to see some movement. Nothing.

Kay felt the same crushing pressure on her chest as that day years ago when she'd opened the door to that uniformed man who had told her Nicholas was gone. *Forever* never had such meaning as it had that night—and as it had right now.

". . . all we could . . . hurting . . . suffer." The vet was telling her something, but she couldn't absorb his words.

"When?" she asked.

"Fifteen minutes ago," the vet said.

The barn went quiet. She felt Kenny's arms around her, lifting her to her feet, guiding her toward the door, past Shawna, who looked small and anxious. *She's so young,* Kay thought, *and now she's not that smart-mouth I deal with in the shops or in the truck.*

Kay glimpsed the deep fear in Shawna's eyes, in the way she crouched, pulling her knees to her chest and pressed against the rough barn wood. *How can I reach someone so walled up inside? I couldn't reach Nicholas, either. Maybe I didn't try hard enough at the time. Maybe I didn't do the right kind of trying. I wish I could reach this girl.*

Kenny was holding the kitchen door open for her. "I've got whiskey in the trailer. I'll go get it."

Kay nodded blindly and went up the steps. The only way she'd get through tonight would be to let Kenny Fargo take over. She'd let him put the bit between her teeth, and go in any direction he thought best. He'd saved her once before. Oh, God, he had to save her again.

Kay knew she had to survive long enough to do something right to rescue that child, the troubled girl huddling in the barn. Her son's only daughter, his only child. She was the last of Nicholas. What was left of her family.

When Kenny returned and handed her a half-filled tumbler, she readily took a large sip. The whiskey-burn down the length of her throat felt good; it made her feel alive. For a short time there was something besides an aching emptiness inside her body.

Shawna stole through the kitchen, her eyes down. Kay let her go without a word. She didn't know what to say after today's session at the therapist's, after the shouting match in the truck, after . . . the gray.

"I'm borrowing Floyd's backhoe in the morning," Kenny said, setting his glass down. "This one's not leaving the ranch. That okay by you?"

Kay nodded.

"You got any place special in mind for her?"

She didn't have to think before she answered. "Along the back trail, just before the rise. There's a boulder on the north side. I'd like her head toward that boulder."

Kenny drained his glass. "You come out around noon. Then we'll say a few words." He walked to the door.

183

"Kenny." Kay wanted him to stay, but when he turned at the sound of her voice, she knew he had to go. It was time for him to grieve, and he did that best alone. "Thank you."

He said nothing as he closed the door behind him.

Kay turned off the lights and walked toward her bedroom. She felt so tired. Yet she knew sleep wouldn't come to set her mind free or let her rest. She was about to close her door, then changed her mind and walked down the hall to Shawna's room.

"Shawna?" she called softly.

Although Shawna didn't answer, Kay heard her move.

"May I come in?"

A drawer slid closed and Kay heard the rustle of sheets.

"Yes," Shawna said. Her voice didn't sound sleepy; it sounded more like she was out of breath.

Kay had a lot to say to the girl she found sitting up in the darkened room, with the moonlight from the window etching her shadow against the wall. But Kay's words sounded paltry, and Shawna's look told her she wasn't getting her message across.

Kay wanted Shawna to know that it wasn't her fault the gray died today without having her person with her. It wasn't anyone's fault.

I've lost this girl, Kay thought as she pressed her fingers against her eyelids. *Will I lose everyone I love before I die?*

Chapter 36

Shawna

After I finish screaming at Kay in the truck, I don't have anything else to say on the ride home from Sacramento. And neither does Kay. Normal silence, right? But as we bump down the long road to the house, I see something that isn't normal.

The barn is flooded with lights. I spot the vet's SUV about the same time the truck screeches to a halt. Kay's out from behind the wheel before I even touch my door handle.

She runs, kicking off her high heels, her hair flying behind her, the clasp lost. She's inside the barn before I can get out of the truck. It's been a freaking long day. I've been thinking hot bath and bed. Now I'm thinking it'll be a freaking long night.

I edge uneasily toward the stall, where I hear Kenny and the vet.

It's the gray. Her tail stretched out long and quiet behind her. I've seen her at the gallop, that tail streaming in the wind. I know she put a high arc in it, showing off her

Arabian side. But now the arc is gone, and along with it, the gray.

Kay sits next to her, her hand on the great strong neck. The gray always rubbed Kay's shoulder from behind, whenever it wanted her touch.

My grandmother is silent, but her body sways. And I hear her, like I've heard others from dark alleys. People hidden in shadows. People crying in pain.

I lean back against the rough planks and slide down onto the straw. I've come to know straw, the way it feels on the end of a pitchfork, the smell of it green and dry, and right now, I crave its prickle on my legs. That will make things feel normal inside the barn tonight. It'll give me something to hate, something to fill up the space inside, that's dark and on the edge of shaky.

"Kay." It's the vet talking to her. "We did all we could for her. But she was hurting too much. We knew you wouldn't want her to suffer."

"When?" Kay's voice is low and flat.

"Fifteen minutes ago. I'm truly sorry. We didn't know when you'd be back." In a while, the vet walks past me. The engine starts and the van drives off.

Fifteen minutes ago the gray was alive, waiting for Kay to come to her. Fifteen minutes ago, I was mouthing off about the shrink and the waste of my time. Fifteen minutes ago the world was different.

I look at Kay. She's as still as her mare, only I know her heart is beating and the mare's is not, and the difference in their stillness is bigger than anything I know. I put my hand where my heart used to be. *Blump, blump.* It's a lonely sound.

"Come on, old girl. I'll take care of the rest." Kenny pulls Kay to her feet and holds her like something precious. "You go on inside." He steers her past me.

I'm alone with the dead gray horse. I push myself up and go to sit by her.

Hey! This is just a horse, Shawna! I shout in my mind. *What's the big deal?*

Fifteen minutes. That's the big deal. Whoever thought a quarter of an hour could make so much difference in the world?

I've never touched anything dead before. But it's not scary. I stroke the Arabian queen's long neck, but I'm having a problem seeing because my eyes are washing out with tears. I never expected to cry over a dead horse. I never expected a lot of things.

I walk into the house and through the kitchen, where Kay and Kenny sit at the kitchen table, sipping dark whiskey. The only sounds are my feet crossing the linoleum.

I'm working on not showing them my wet eyes. Besides, I'm not ready to talk to Kay, and for sure, she's not ready to talk to me. Vegas was hard, but it was easier than this. *I never cried in Vegas.*

The bed is wide and I stretch my length across its middle, letting my legs dangle over the side. I stare at the ceiling and I listen to the night sounds coming on. Tonight the coyotes aren't talking. Owls take over the dark air. I never heard an owl before I came to Kay's, and its lonely question is always a surprise. It's my question. How in the hell can a stupid thing with feathers and big eyes ask a

187

question, anyway? Maybe owls aren't stupid. Maybe I'm the stupid thing without feathers that asks bird questions.

Who? Who? Who?

Who in the hell am I?

Tonight is real different. Kay doesn't do her kitchen-cooking-on-the-table-dinner-at-seven routine. I'm on the bed listening to owls! Kenny? He's doing something about the gray, and I don't want to know. I only know I'm feeling maggots in my stomach.

Fifteen minutes.

Fifteen lousy minutes.

And here he comes, even before the shakes start. My snaggle-toothed critter. Crawling from the end of the bed.

"Go away! I don't want you here tonight."

"But you do. Tonight you really need me."

I look at his greedy eyes. He knows I'm down. He knows. And I do, too.

I take the razor blade out and begin to unwrap it. Take it slow. Don't rush. Maybe he'll slink away if I don't hurry. Unfold. Unfold. The thin, icy metal slides onto my palm. It weighs nothing, but my hand grows tired from holding it.

"Shawna. Come on, Sweetie. Nice and deep," Monster coos.

I'm surprised at the blood this time. It's more than usual. It's a lot, actually. I grab the sheet and press hard against my ankle.

"Shawna?"

It's Kay's voice at the door. Monster skulks away. He's pissed. Too bad.

"May I come in?"

What the hell, it's her house. Why does she always ask if she can come in? I sit up and tuck the razor blade into the drawer and pull the sheet sideways so she can't see what I've done. "Yes."

The door swings in. She's still in the meet-the-shrink-suit, but her hair fans across her shoulders and she's in bare feet.

"I'm sorry," Kay says.

My eyebrows shoot to heaven. I stop myself from saying, "Huh?"

"You can't blame yourself any more than I can." She walks in and sits on the edge of the bed. "She was a good horse and she had someone to love her, her whole life."

She takes a moment to press her fingers against her eyes, then she looks up. "That's more than a lot of people get, right, Shawna?"

I nod. I'm totally not understanding any of this. Why isn't she like, pounding on my head and telling me what a creep I am for being here, for messing up her perfect life, for dragging her off to some shrink, when she should have been with her gray?

It's good I'm going back to Vegas. There I know where I stand.

189

Chapter 37

Shawna

It's Saturday afternoon, and my crowded social calendar shows I've got one major event to look forward to—Marta's sleepover. I'm wearing socks all the time since Wednesday night. My ankle hurts, and once in a while if I catch it right, it bleeds.

Damn Monster.

I soaked the sheets and did a load of laundry while Kay was out with Kenny that next day. She asked me to go along and I wanted to, but the sheets . . . .

"What time do you have to be at Marta's?" Kay's coming from the barn and I'm passing her on my way to see Magic, since I won't be here tomorrow.

"Seven," I say.

"Floyd's in the hospital. He had a fall, Kenny tells me. Give his horses some oats and check their water, will you?"

So old Floyd dropped off his perch. Magic should feel pretty happy about that.

Magic comes from across the field and rubs his head against my shoulder.

"You act more like Buster sometimes than you do a horse, you know that? Here." I hold out his apple and the vitamins.

In only a couple of months, Magic looks like some other horse. I'm thinking how I can get him to Vegas, maybe board him someplace.

Yeah, Shawna, you got so much money for that. The savings from my twenty-dollar-a-week salary has grown to about a hundred, but I know what boarding fees are here, and in Vegas they gotta be a ton more.

"I'll fit you into Tuan's dump. How does that sound?" I can't imagine him or me anywhere near that place. Seems funny that Las Vegas isn't a fit anymore. *Fit or no fit, I'm going. Don't have anyplace else to go.*

Magic tosses his head.

"Yeah, I gotta call the old lady tomorrow. Gotta make plans for my return to the nest." I climb onto the fence. "Wanna go out on the trail?'

Magic sidles up and I climb onto his bare back. "Now don't go crazy on me, okay? I'm still new at this horse riding business."

Magic starts at a slow walk across the field. I unlatch the gate and he pushes it open, then he waits for me to kick it closed before heading down the road that borders Floyd's shack. He cuts across the pasture in front and winds down the path that leads to the trail beyond Kay's barn. At the bottom of the rise, he stops. The large mound of fresh earth marks the grave for Kay's horse, the boulder is her headstone.

I lean forward over Magic and lay my head against his sleek, black neck.

She was a good horse.

"Are you talking to me again?"

Seems you need to hear something.

"And what do I need to hear from a horse?"

Same as you need to hear from inside your heart.

"Let's ride, okay? I got a lot of thinking to do."

He climbs the rise and follows the trail to the creek.

"Tonight I gotta go to something called a sleepover with a bunch of loonies and a troll. What was I thinking when I said yes?"

That you were lonely.

"Say what?"

Come on, Shawna, face it. You come to me to talk, but you need some of your own kind to hang with. I know.

"Why don't you just walk and leave the talking to me, okay?"

I've known a lot of your kind, but you are one untrusting human, I can tell you that.

We circle back to the property and then to Floyd's. I give the horses a double ration of grass hay and fresh water.

"Bye, Magic." I rub his forehead.

Go to your sleepover. And for a change, stop being such a grump and pushing everybody away.

He lowers his head so I can reach behind his ears.

While you're there, you might see if you can smile a few times too, okay?

"Mind your own business!"

I am.

This is way too nuts, this talking to Magic, but as I'm walking back to Kay's, I think about all he's said, or would have said if he really could. Maybe I am a little lonely. I'm not as busy as I used to be in Las Vegas. I'll drop that lonely crap once I'm back there, taking care of Mom again. I'll be too tired to be lonely.

When we drive up to Marta's, the house looks like it's open for a sale or something. All the lights are on inside, and the driveway has two cars and a truck lined up to the street. That truck! It's Casey's. Is he coming to the sleep-over, too? I glance at Kay.

"I see Casey's here," she says. "Guess the rumors are true."

"Rumors?" I say before I catch myself.

"He's seeing one of the Dumont girls."

The Dumont girl? *Who the hell is the Dumont girl? And why don't I know this rumor? Why didn't Marta say something while we were talking the other day? Why does it matter, anyway? Right. It doesn't.*

"Are you getting out?" Kay asks.

I shrug.

"Shawna?"

"If I don't want to stay . . ." I can't believe I'm saying this.

"Call me. I'll pick you up," Kay says before I can take it back. "But I think you'll have a great time. Marta's mom, Jenny Kilpatrick, and I are old friends. She's a very nice person."

Kay stares at the house and disconnects from me, like she's suddenly gone somewhere else.

"Well?" she asks focusing on me again.

"Okay." *Do a thing that scares you right away and look like you know what you're doing. It works when you lift stuff off a shelf. It works when you get on Magic. It'll work now.* I push open the truck door and step down with my sleeping bag under my arm. I look at Kay for a moment.

"Call me if you need to, but go in thinking that you won't."

She sounds like Magic. I know she's part horse. I close the door and walk toward the house fast, like I actually want to get there. Behind me I hear Kay's truck pull out, and I think about turning and running after her. *No. You will not turn and run. You never turn and run—unless the cops are after you.*

I'm about to knock at the door when it opens and there's Casey. *Who's more surprised, him or me?*

"Hi, Shawna. Heard you were coming." Casey steps aside and holds the door open until I walk past. "Don't bite any of the girls, okay?"

I have something to say to him, but he's already down the driveway by the time I turn around.

"Shawna!" Marta pokes her head out of the kitchen. "Come on. The pizza is here and we're diving in."

I tighten my grip on the sleeping bag and bite my lower lip. I'm not good at the girly-girl thing. I know I'm going to hate this.

194

As I walk across Marta's fun-house floor, I hear Magic in my head. . . . *Stop being such a grump and pushing everybody away.*

For you, Magic, I'll give it a try.

Chapter 38

Kay

Kay watched the exchange between Casey and Shawna at the front door. From the truck, even in the dim evening lighting, she could see the tension in Shawna's stance and the expression on Casey's face. Not his usual nice-kid expression. Kay'd known him since he was born, but tonight the seventeen-year-old had a whole different look than her usual Sunday Boy.

She sighed and made a U-turn. At the stop sign, she crossed her fingers and held them high. "Make this party a breakthrough for Shawna, okay?" Kay knew how girls that age could shut out the "newbie," but Marta had made the invitation and, knowing Marta's mother like she did, Kay believed Marta was sincere.

Jenny Kilpatrick had been Nic's first serious girlfriend, and if all had gone according to plan . . . Kay laughed out loud. "And what plan would that be?" *Wouldn't Shawna be surprised to know that she could have been named Marta Stone?*

Shawna's the loose canon, so tonight's success de-

pends a lot on how she acts, on what she says and does.
Kay shook her head and made a right turn toward the hospital a mile away.

She'd made up her mind that while she was in Sweet River, she'd check up on Floyd. The old coot was killing himself with alcohol, but she remembered how he was before he fell into the bottle. She'd visit him and maybe talk business if he was up to it.

The parking lot was almost empty. She pulled in front of the main entrance, climbed out of the truck, and pushed the glass doors open.

"Evening, Kay." It was Ted Holt. He volunteered for the night shift at the Information Desk.

"Hi, Ted. I came to see Floyd."

"Room 110 to the right. His son's with him right now."

"Thanks." Kay walked through the lobby and down the corridor to the room. The door stood open, so she walked in.

The first bed was empty and the curtain was pulled around the second one near the windows. A tall man she recognized from years ago slumped in a chair against the wall.

"Victor?" she asked.

The man looked up, his face drawn and tired.

"It's Kay Stone. I came to see your father."

"You're too late. Dad's gone. He died about ten minutes ago."

She couldn't say, "I'm sorry." And she didn't have any other words to use, so she stood next to the man in the chair and said nothing.

Victor looked about the same as the last time she'd talked to him, about a year ago when he'd visited Floyd. Slightly gray at the temples, a small paunch, and sad blue eyes. But if she looked past the years, he became the lanky kid clamoring outside their kitchen door, waiting for Nic to play. Floyd and Nell's oldest son almost lived with the Stones. Later, Floyd complained she was stealing him away, but he never forgot that she'd saved this boy's life the night the rest of his family died.

"Come outside with me," she said at last, taking his arm and leading him into the corridor. "Let's find some coffee and a place to talk."

The cafeteria was closed, but the coffee urn was still on and half full. She filled two Styrofoam cups and sat across from Victor. "I can help with the arrangements if you want."

He shook his head. "Dad didn't want anything. Cremation and burial next to Mom and the kids."

Kay sipped her coffee.

"It was a bad fall. Too much booze." Victor swiped his eyes.

"Will you be here for a while to take care of your father's business?"

He nodded. "But most of it's done. Dad sold out last month and was planning to move closer to me. I just have to pack some personal things before the new people come in."

"I wish I'd known he was selling. I was interested." Kay felt awkward talking about real estate now, but she'd always thought she'd buy Floyd's and expand her stables.

She'd talked to him about an option years ago. And now that she was in a position to make the deal, he'd sold it without giving her a chance.

"And the horses?" she asked.

"They're gone along with the property. Dad dumped everything at once."

"Who bought the place?" she asked.

"Out-of-towners. I haven't had time to go over the details." He studied his coffee, and then looked up at her. "I'm going to the house tomorrow, take out what I want, and then I'm gone. That place doesn't hold a lot of good memories, you know?"

"I know," Kay said.

"You've been in one place too long." Victor said. "You know all the stories."

Kay nodded, but at the same time she couldn't imagine where else on this planet she could call home.

"I know you looked after Dad when he took to drinking. He told me." Victor smiled, but it was a sad, lonely smile. "When he sobered up, he told me what you and Kenny did for him."

"I always thought of Floyd as my friend, so what Kenny or I did was what we wanted to do."

They walked back to Room 110 together. Before Victor went inside, he took both of her hands in his. "Thank you for everything, Kay."

Kay strode past the Information Desk before Ted Holt looked up from his newspaper.

Outside, she turned the truck toward home like she turned a horse toward the barn. Just like the horse, she

hoped her truck would find its way home without her paying attention.

She needed to talk to Kenny.

Chapter 39

Shawna

I step into Marta's kitchen not knowing what to expect, and a good thing, too, because I'd never have come in here if I'd suspected what I'd find in this room. Marta, of course, in an oversized T-shirt down to her knees, but also the two blonds—the twins I'd seen hanging out with her and Casey at school.

Then there's the mom. Smiling like she's been waiting for me all her life, she grabs me and pulls me to her before I can duck. "Shawna! I'm so happy you could come. Marta's told me all about you, and I've been so looking forward to meeting you."

I'm being hugged! And I'm like, totally freaking. *No touching. No touching!* That's my rule. It isn't something I'm accustomed to, and I'm not at all sure I can take it.

I must look out of it when she backs off. Still holding onto my shoulders, she examines me like she's found something, but she's not sure exactly what.

"I'm sorry, I must seem a little crazy, but I grew up with your father. My name's Jenny." She gives my shoulders a squeeze. "Nic was my first boyfriend. I just think it's so wonderful that you're at Kay's. She must be so proud of you."

My gawd, is the woman going to go on forever? *And what is this about my father?* I must have a really weird look on my face, somewhere between shocked and sick, because this Jenny person is eyeing me like I'm a crazy who needs watching.

I look past her at the giggling twins as they try pulling pizza slices from the box. Marta is smiling at me, her T-shirt message jiggling across her boobs: LOVE BUNNY. I think I'm going to be sick.

"Come on, Shawna. Dig in. It's the Double Monster with everything!" Marta says.

It's my chance to escape her mom, the hugger. I take it and tear off a slice, then fill my mouth with hot cheese, pepperoni, olives, you name it. I'm taking the Double Monster down tonight. If I can take two monsters at a time, I should be able to take on my regular one anytime. I chew pizza until it's in tiny, mushy pieces. I swallow and wash it down with a huge gulp of Coke, which I hate. But when in Rome . . . make that Sweet River.

"Okay, girls. I'm off to the movies. I'll be back about ten. Marta, you charged my cell?" Jenny asks.

Marta nods.

"Have fun! Be happy!" Jenny calls as she closes the front door behind her.

Have fun. Be happy. I'm chewing on those ideas as hard as I'm chewing on the Double Monster. At the same time I'm looking at Marta, wondering how she'd look if she were my father's daughter. That leads to wondering how I'd look if I were Jenny's daughter? Like a troll? I bite down and tear off another piece of pizza.

Marta must have taken Martha Stewart classes. She's smiling, pouring more Coke when a glass is empty, offering napkins. *How come she isn't as trollish tonight? How come when she looks at me, it's with straight-on, non-ferret eyes? And she's definitely stopped smelling bad.*

"So, Marta says you're in her AP classes," one of the twins says. "That's why I never see you. I'm not AP material." She laughs and toasts her twin with her Coke.

"Me, neither." The look-alike smirks. "So what's it like being smart?"

"What's it like being dumb?" It's out of my mouth before I know it.

"Hey! Shawna, you gotta be nice tonight, all right?" Marta's Love Bunny is hopping on her chest and she's turning red in the face.

. . . for a change stop being such a grump and pushing everybody away.

I can't shake Magic's advice. It's still echoing in my head. I hold up my hands like I'm surrendering. "Sorry. I don't want to talk about school, okay? Let's talk about something else."

"How about Ca-sey?" "Me, neither" tilts her chin and smiles, first at her sister and then at me, splitting the syllables in Casey's name equally between us.

"Deirdre, you're a troublemaker. I told you—" her sister throws her crust and hits Deirdre in the chest; then she turns to me. "You know I'm seeing Casey, right?"

"That's not any of my business. I don't even know who *you* are, so who you go with isn't something I'd care about."

I grab another slice of pizza, taking a big bite. If I keep my mouth full of food, I can't talk—something I'm not going to be good at tonight.

"My name's Deanna, spelled with two *N*'s." She holds up her left hand.

"This is Casey's ring."

Since my mouth is full, I shrug.

"What's that supposed to mean?" Deanna asks.

"It means I don't give a sh—"

Marta is between Deanna and me in a flash. "Come on. My CD player's in my room." She pulls me through the kitchen door and down the hall. "You like Rap, don't you?"

"I despise Rap." I'm in no mood to cooperate.

"Shawna." Marta says my name and her voice pleads. "Please."

. . . for a change stop being such a grump and pushing everybody away.

"Play whatever you want. Rap is fine." I'm tired of this sleepover already and I've been here less than an hour.

Deirdre and Deanna travel together as a package. They come into Marta's bedroom together and spread their identical sleeping bags side by side on the floor. I think I've got them sorted out. Deirdre's nose has a small bump in the center and Deanna's doesn't. If I study their noses, I'll know which one is which.

I retrieve my bag from the kitchen, and when I come

back Chino Lite is blasting the wallpaper loose. D and D
are doing an imitation of a dance, looking like two of
Buster's fleas on a night out.

This is too weird! I kick off my shoes and squat on
my bag. *How long does this song last?* Still, I move to the
beat. Chino Lite is my number-one favorite. Marta has
good taste in music.

Marta joins the twins and hauls me to my feet. I shake
my head no, but she's got my wrists. Short of breaking her
arm, I'm not getting free.

"Come on," she shouts. "I know you have some good
moves."

Ha! She doesn't have a clue what good moves are. I
haven't slid around the floor since I left Vegas, but the
moves come back: slide to the right, go down and circle,
punch and kick and . . . now I forget the moves and let the
dance flow through me. I've got a good sweat up. It's like
I'm back where I should be, outside the hottest joint on
the old strip, lost in the tunes.

There're things I miss about that town. Dancing is
one. On the nights when Mom wasn't coming home, I'd
cut out of Tuan's and head downtown. There, lights sprin-
kled over me, and music and slots clattered up and down
the streets. How'd I get stuck here in Hicksville? I hop on
my toes and spin, go around, elbow out, head out . . . .

When the music stops, I flop onto my bag. After
Chino Lite, the silence rings like an apartment house
buzzer in my ears. When I look up, the two D's and Marta
are staring down at me. "What?"

"Where did you learn that?" Marta asks. Her voice
sounds like she's just seen Britney Spears in person.

The two D's have their arms crossed over their chests. "Church."

"Can you teach me?" Marta has returned to golden retriever mode.

"Only if you're a fast learner. I'm leaving pretty soon."

"Why?" Marta sits next to me, her Love Bunny brushing against my arm. She has a look I don't understand, but it's something between "I failed my math test!" and "My mother has cancer."

"It's time." I'm not getting into "my grandmother hates me, my mother's broke, yadda, yadda, yadda."

"Well, that sucks, you know?" Marta says. "But could you . . .?"

"Yeah. Yeah. I'll show you some steps." I stand and Marta powers up Chino Lite again. "Go low and turn. Try again. Okay. Okay. Nice. Now, work your shoulders." I stand in front of Marta and show her how to dip and sway, so her head and the top part of her body flow to the beat.

Deirdre—I check out her nose—yes, for sure Deirdre, tries to follow, but she's definitely not got the moves in her. Fish in the bottom of a boat do hip-hop way better than Deirdre. Deanna pretends she's not interested, but I catch her looking up at us. She's not kidding me. She wants to learn, and bad.

Marta is a fast learner and she's good. I give her a high five before I remember who she is and where I am.

"I gotta stop. I'm bushed." I fall back on my sleeping bag.

Marta lowers the volume on the CD and crashes next

to me. "You are good, Shawna. You have to enter the spring dance contest. You'll win!"

I shrug.

"I mean it. It's a big thing, you know? You get clothes, you get money, and . . . you ready?" Marta sits back on her golden retriever haunches. "A Chino Lite CD!"

I want to shrug, but I can't. I can win that contest, hands down. I'm getting ready to ask more about it when my friend Deanna, No Bump on her Nose, asks:

"So when do you go back to Las Vegas?" She wants me out of good old Sweet River. Casey doth protest too much. I know all I have to do is show some interest and he'll dump this little clone. Sweet little Deanna knows it too.

"Whenever I'm ready." I'm not giving her any information.

Deanna pulls out her overnight bag and begins filing her nails. "Deirdre, what interesting little bit of news did you hear today?"

Deirdre looks blank and fiddles with her hair.

"You know, the story about how Shawna is seeing that psychologist in Sacramento?"

What does Mom always say? "Expect the worst, then when the bad comes along you can handle it." I should have been ready for this one. I'm going Sweet River soft again. No. Now I'm down to squishy.

"That's none of your business, Deanna." Marta's voice surprises me. It sounds hard as rock.

"It's none of anybody's business," I say, standing up and grabbing my bag.

"Besides, it's not true." And it wasn't. I saw a therapist, not a psychologist.

I'm so out of this place, that before the front door closes behind me, in my head, I'm already packed and on the bus back to Vegas. I'm going to Kay's, call Mom, get myself a ticket, and then it's "Adios, Sweet River."

I sling my bag over my shoulder and pick my way down the hill, past the park and into town. The stores are dark and the streets are empty, except for a couple of cars in front of the Howling Dog Saloon.

I walk past the saloon and look in. Nobody inside looks familiar or like someone I'd want to ask for a lift, so I hike back to the park and sit on the bottom of the plastic slide, my sleeping bag across my lap. *Now what?* I'm tired, so I lay my head on my bag and close my eyes. *If I was sticking around, I'd get those stupid clones. Then they'd know some real pain. But right now all I want is a bed.*

"Shawna?"

I'm almost out of my skin by the time I jump up and face Marta. "Damn, Marta, you scared me! What do you want now?"

"I'm sorry, Shawna. Please come back to the house. They didn't mean what they said. They're like totally jealous of you, you know."

I point to myself, surprised.

"Yes, you. You're smarter and prettier than they are, and everybody knows Casey's only dating Deanna to get your attention."

"He's like, wasting his time. I'm so not interested."

Marta sits on the grass cross-legged and stares at me, like she's waiting for me to say more. "I'm sorry I asked them to come, but they swore they just wanted to get to know you. It was stupid of me to believe them." She plucks at the grass and piles it on her thigh. "I'm not too swift that way, you know? I always believe what people tell me."

"You wouldn't last long in Vegas."

She sort of laughs and piles more grass bits on her leg. "So why the shrink?" she asks, finally.

"It's really none of your business."

"I went to a therapist once," Marta says, "after my dad left. Me and my mom went. It helped." Marta looks across the park. "It's nothing to be ashamed of."

"Who says I'm ashamed? What is wrong with every friggin' person in this town? Do they have to know everything about everybody?" I slam my sleeping bag with my fist, wishing it were Deanna or Deirdre.

"Nothing's wrong with being interested," Marta says.

"Butt out of my life and take your charmin' duo with you." I heft my bag under my arm and start toward town again.

"Where are you going, Shawna? You can't walk back to your grandmother's now!" Marta catches up with me and grabs my arm. "Wait! I called Casey. He's on his way to get you."

I want to hit her. Why does she muck around in my life? But it's already too late; Casey's truck is rolling to a stop at the curb.

Chapter 40

Shawna

Casey walks up to us, takes my sleeping bag without saying a thing, then drops it in the back of his truck. He opens the passenger door and waits like a patient sheepherder for the last of his flock to straggle in.

He drops Marta at her house. And while she's standing out front, waving at us, the door opens and a twin's head pops out. Now I'm the one who's smiling—the biggest and widest I can manage—and I'm waving back like I'm off to Paris. Ah, life can be good.

"I'll hear about this later tonight," Casey says, as he pulls away.

"I didn't ask for the ride."

"No, but I'll wager you tricked Marta into asking."

"You have an ego the size of a planet, do you know that? I don't want anything from you, except to leave me alone." I scoot as far against my door as I can, and scrunch down into the seat. I can barely see over the dash.

It's a fast trip down the highway, a skidding turn onto Kay's road, and a grinding stop a few feet from the red house. But before I can escape, Casey's across the seat, pinning me against the door. I'm not breathing and my hands would be shaking if they had the room, but he's pressed against me so hard, there's no space between us for the shakes.

"I don't like people touching me!" I shout.

"Is that 'cause you're not human?" His face is inches from mine.

"Guys make me sick."

"Guys? Or is it just me?"

"Both."

His lips touch mine. I clench my teeth and try to pull back, but there's no room for escape. He mashes his mouth against mine, forcing my head into the metal corner of the truck.

He eases back, still pinning me against the door. "Kiss me, Shawna."

"Go kiss your girlfriend. Leave me alone."

"I've tried leaving you alone. But for some reason I can't." He smiles.

It's a long, slow smile that has the pull of a strong undertow. I'm losing my footing, and if I'm not careful I'll disappear under its force.

"I've got you tucked under my heart."

Then he kisses me. Casey's lips are warm and firm against mine. I hear the rush of cool, dark water and I'm drifting, daydreaming. My arms cling to Magic's strong neck, and Casey is riding alongside. His smile reassures me that I'm going in the right direction.

Up? Down? Forward? Backward? I don't know. Magic is saying, *This is the way, Shawna*. Casey's smile says, *Listen to him*.

Then Casey isn't pressing against me anymore. Magic disappears and the water drains away, leaving me like something washed up at low tide, my back heavy against the door. I keep my eyes clenched shut and listen as Casey climbs out the driver's side and drags my sleeping bag from the back. I hear the soft thud of it landing on the porch, then the crunch of gravel under his boots, and the scrape of my door opening.

He touches my arm and I want to let him, but I still can't do that. No touching is a rule—my rule. I jerk away and climb out. Without looking back at him, I run into the house, letting the door slam behind me. Outside, Casey spins his truck around and drives away really fast.

The shakes have got me. I'm holding on the best I can, but I've got to call Mom right away. I've got to get out of here now.

Before I can make it to the phone, Kay calls from the kitchen. "Shawna?" She pokes her head into the living room. "What's wrong?"

Leave me alone I want to scream, but for some reason I can't. I wrap my arms around myself and pin my hands under my armpits. This way she can't see me shake.

"How did you get home?"

Kenny comes up behind her, and I try staring him down. I try making him go away, but he's Kay's backup and he's not going anywhere, not even if I was a pit bull with rabies.

"Casey." It's not a whisper, but it's not full volume either.

Kay steps toward me. I move back.

"I want to call my mom."

"Shawna . . ." Kay reaches out her hand, and then lets it fall to her side. "Use my office phone."

The office with its walls of books feels safe when I close the door and lean against it. There's too much in my head, too much swirling inside me for me to pick up the phone at first. I stand propped against the solid wood and listen to my breathing, feel the air go in and out of my body.

What if I had to think about breathing the same way I do to write essays or curry horses? I couldn't manage to think about inhaling and exhaling all day and all night and still do anything else. And right now, I'm having trouble turning that job back to autopilot. I have to tell myself to breathe in, breathe out.

What was Casey trying to prove? Breathe in. *Why did I let him come so close to me?* Breathe out. *He kissed me.* Breathe in. *I kissed him back.* Breathe out. Breathe in.

I've seen enough of what kissing is all about. I've seen the sweethearts come and go. I've locked them out of the only room with a door and a lock—and sat on the linoleum or in the bathtub or in the shower with towels wrapped around me, waiting. Breathing in. Breathing out.

I kissed Casey back.

Sweet River soft.

I can deal with the phone now, and I'd better get on it. The clock says it's after nine and Mom's out and about by

213

ten. I take the paper with her number out of my pocket and smooth it on Kay's desk. I punch in the numbers and wait. One ring. Two.

"Hello."

"Hi, Mom."

It's one beat too long before she answers. Someone is there with her.

"Oh, yes. How are you?"

How am I? The question hammers the inside of my skull.

"Hold on."

I hear some shuffling and footsteps. A door closes and her voice comes back on the line. "I didn't expect to hear from you tonight, Sweetie. What's up?"

I had the words ready to say before I heard her voice, before she answered the phone as Jackie instead of Mom. But now, my brain is mute. It's not talking to me, and I'm not talking to her.

It's the same as the night Dylan came on to me. When I unlocked the bathroom door and she hit me and called me a slut. It was my fault. All mine.

"Shawna? Why are you calling? Just to breathe in my ear?"

"I'm . . . not sure I'm coming back to Las Vegas."

"You little . . . ! You're calling me at a time like . . . Never mind. What changed your mind? Kay?"

"She—"

"Why don't you have her tell you how much she wanted you in the beginning? How she pushed for me to have an abortion? Now that you're all grown up, she's changed her tune, right? Well, screw her, and screw you!"

And with a click, Mom's gone. Jackie's in a room someplace with someone, and I'm in a canyon of books.

Breathing in. Breathing out.

Chapter 41

Kay

Kay drove back to the ranch from the hospital and went straight to Kenny's trailer. She rapped at his door and it opened before she'd stepped back. "You expecting a visitor? Or do you stand by that door all night?"

Kenny tucked in his shirt. "A little of both. How's Floyd?"

She didn't need to answer. Her face gave her away. "Can you come to the house for a cup of coffee? Floyd sold his ranch without telling us. I wanted to run some ideas by you, about talking to the new owners. I'm thinking about maybe making them an offer."

They walked to the house and Kay plugged in the coffeemaker. "I saw Victor at the hospital tonight." She pulled cookies out of the jar and spread them on a plate.

"How's the boy holding up?"

"He's no boy anymore. Same age as Nicholas would be. Thirty-five! Can you believe that? He's coming over tomorrow to pack whatever he wants from the house. I thought I'd ask him about the new people. Get a feel for how to approach them. Or even if there's a chance they'll want to sell. I didn't want to talk business. I mean, his father . . . it must have been hard for Victor, even after all these years of Floyd's drinking. He doesn't have any other relatives."

"He havin' a service?"

"No. I'll go to the cemetery next week and put in some flowers. Floyd will be buried next to Nell and the kids." Kay listened to the coffee percolate and smelled the fresh richness that slowly filled the room. "Nell and the kids," she whispered to herself.

Even while Floyd was building the new house around her, Nell would make fresh coffee every morning about ten, then she'd lean over the fence and yell, "Kay Stone! It's coffee!" And Kay would put down the saddle or hang up the bridle she'd been polishing, and climb over the fence. Nell started the tradition of their daily twenty minutes at her table, exchanging stories about Nic and Vic, their terrible ten-year-olds who were always up to some kind of mischief.

How did a person get mud stains out of white socks after they'd been stashed under a bed for a month? And did Kay know about the firecrackers? Floyd confiscated a whole shoe box full.

Floyd and Nell's Ben, only three, scooted across the floor after his favorite wind-up toy, while Darcy, the girl with more curls than a poodle, darted in and out. Floyd always passed through at least once to get a cup of coffee before he went back to work on the house.

That last time Kay and Nell sat together, Floyd was on

a ladder, putting the final coat of white paint on the siding. The next time Kay saw him, his life and his newly painted house were ashes.

The light on the coffee pot flashed red. Done.

"How about the horses? They part of the deal Floyd made?" Kenny bit into a cookie.

"Yes. I'll ask about including them in my offer." Kay filled two coffee mugs and sat across from Kenny. "Shawna's got one of them looking healthy, and it might be good for her to have the responsibility of a horse of her own. What do you think?"

"Casey tells me she's over there with that black one every Sunday. Says she talks to him. Did you know that?"

Kay laughed. "No. But my apple supply dwindles more every week. If she's feeding and talking to a horse, that's two things she does that don't worry me. Everything else has me walking a narrow ledge." She warmed her hands against the coffee mug and stared into the dark brew.

"Shawna's at her sleepover, so keep your fingers crossed. I'm praying this little socializing will put a chink in that armor of hers. Maybe she'll start talking to people and not just that horse."

"You going back to see the doc next week?"

"We made an appointment, but I'm not sure Shawna's going to cooperate. I'm hoping she'll go willingly . . . I don't feel right about forcing her. She's got to want to do this." Her elbows on the table, Kay let her head rest in both hands. "Still, I'm the adult, and I should decide what's right for her." She looked up. "What should I do?"

"Take her to the doctor. She needs more than a sleepover to kick loose from whatever's wrapped around her innards."

"Maybe I need more help, too." She stood and paced between the table and the sink. "I'm in way over my head."

"It seems that way. But you been there before. Do what you gotta do, and you'll rise up to the surface." He smiled his brown, snaggletooth smile at her. "I'll give you a boost if I see you runnin' out of air."

Kay gripped his shoulder and he laid his hand over hers. "What would I do without you, old man?"

The front door slammed and tires spun in the dirt. Kay heard a motor revving, and then roaring off down the road. "Shawna?" She hurried into the living room where her granddaughter stood, hands shaking, eyes wild. "What's wrong?"

Shawna shook her head and folded her arms across her chest, tucking her hands under her armpits.

"How did you get home?" Kay had a lot more questions to ask. What happened at the sleepover? What's wrong with you? Are you sick? Hurt? But fear had the words trapped below her throat.

"Casey." It was a whimper. The sound of a terrified pup.

Kay wanted more than anything to hold Shawna close to her, gather her into her arms, and let her know that she was safe. Kay stepped forward and Shawna retreated, keeping the same distance between them.

"I want to call my mom."

"Shawna—" Kay reached out her hand, then let it fall to her side. *Don't push her. She may need her mother, no matter what kind of mother Jackie is. She may need to go home.*

Home. That's what she told Dr. Lubell. I want to go home. So she did mean Las Vegas, as opposed to here? She's asking to call her mother, so maybe I was right about Vegas, but I'd hoped . . . . "Use my office phone."

Kay waited until Shawna walked into the office and closed the door, then she turned to face Kenny, who stood close at her back. "I feel like I can hardly breathe. Like I'm running out of air." She fell against his chest and let him hold her.

Chapter 42

Shawna

After that wonderful conversation with Jackie, I stretch out on my bed. I'll stare at the ceiling and wait for the night to slip away. I'll take a trip in my mind to clean out my head, dump Jackie someplace along a roadside, and drive away without looking back. She'll disappear— a woman, a figure, a speck, nothing.

Monster doesn't take much time coming. He slides up on the foot of my bed and squats. His greedy eyes take up most of his face, and he gives me his best pointy-toothed smile.

"Get outta here," I say, but there's no power in my voice.

He scoots forward.

"I told you. Leave me alone." I'm not letting him boss me around. He's a toad, even worse than that. I look him in the eye. "You're not even real, you creep." But it's like I don't have enough energy to make him hear me. I can hardly hear myself.

"Now. Now, Shawna," his voice wheedles. "What is real?"

"Me! I'm real."

"A real what? Girl? Granddaughter? Say, how about a real daughter with a real mother and father?"

I want to kill him. Grab him by his fat throat, and squeeze until his toad eyes pop out onto the floor and roll around like marbles.

"I know what you're thinking, Sweetie."

"Shut up! Shut up! Shut up!" I clap my hands over my ears, but *Sweetie, Sweetie* rings in my head. Mom's voice. Jackie's voice. The small click and the emptiness of the line strung for miles between Vegas and Sweet River.

I wish I could be five again. I wish she would prop me up on pillows, like she did then, and feed me ice cream again. I would lick the spoon clean and she'd laugh, I'd laugh. And nobody would come to take her out and leave me all alone.

"I'm here, Shawna," Monster coos. "You saw what happened when you were nice and cozy with those girls tonight. And what about that Sunday Boy, Casey? Can't let them in, Shawna. You can't trust anybody but me."

Don't get the shakes. Don't get the shakes.

"I don't want *you*!" I scream, but the words dribble down my chin and soak into the sheets.

"You don't want anyone, Sweetie. And nobody wants you either."

"No!" I sit up and slide my hands under my butt. *Get it together.*

"Where's Daddy? He split the minute you were born. Mommy? She's a busy one. Lots of people more important

222

than you to spend her time with. And how about old Granny? Now you know even *she* didn't want you before you were born. Do you think she wants you now?"

He waits, a smug look drawing his face up tight. "I don't think so," he sing-songs as he scoots even closer. "Oh, and how about that Sunday Boy? You think he'll be around again soon? Not!"

I can feel his breath on my face. The loamy smell that used to be Marta's gags me. Maybe it never belonged to her. Maybe it was Monster in my face all that time. He's not a toad at all. He's The Troll, smothering me with his stench.

I pull out the nightstand drawer and reach for the tissue-wrapped blade. But even as my fingers touch the sharp edge, I know its power is ended. Monster knows it too. He's heard it in my voice. He's seen it in my face. The bottle of small white pills hides at the back of the drawer. I dump them onto my palm and lie down. I'm cold. I pull up the sheet and the blanket to my chin, but I'm okay now. I feel better and stronger. I'm quiet inside and I'm not in the least shaky. Now I have a plan.

One pill. Two. Three.

They're hard to swallow without water, but I'm shaking too much to get up and find my way into the kitchen. I fill my mouth with saliva.

Four. Five. Six.

He's patting me on the head, smoothing my hair away from my forehead. "Nice Monster. Good Monster," he's crooning.

Who's he calling Monster? Me? I'm the Monster? I'm

the one who's kept myself safe and can't any longer? Won't any longer?

Seven. I can't count anymore.

So who am I putting to sleep? Him? Me? Both? I'll take him down right now and get it over with.

I lunge.

Chapter 43

Kay

Kay stayed in the kitchen after Kenny left. She sat at the table and picked at the cookie crumbs on the plate, just stirring them into patterns. Shawna hadn't come back to tell her about the phone call to Jackie, but Kay had heard her go to her room.

Now what, she wondered. *I can go in and talk to her. I can ask when she'd like to leave. Maybe I should wait until morning. Let her sleep. This has been a terrible night for her. Ha! Make that for all of us. Even poor Kenny looked exhausted when he walked out the door.*

She'd had terrible nights before. Lonely nights, sitting here at this table. And it looked like there were more to come. Once Shawna left, her life would go back to what it used to be. And what kind of life was that?

It had only been two months since the girl came, and Kay couldn't imagine how she'd manage without her. Her *Bad Ass Attitude* T-shirt had gone from offensive, to not as bad as others she'd seen in the halls of Sweet River High, to a part of the white load in the weekly laundry.

What would she and Buster do every afternoon, without the run to the school to pick up Shawna? And what about going shopping? Or watching her with the horses in the barn?

Kay carried the mugs to the sink. *There's nothing I can do to keep her here if she doesn't want to stay. Jackie's irresponsible, but she's Shawna's legal guardian.*

"Nic. I need you more everyday."

She went to her room, showered, and pulled her nightgown over her head. She desperately needed to sleep. Tomorrow she'd talk things out with Shawna; then see Vic about the out-of-towners who would become her new neighbors. She'd try and talk to them about the property, see about the horses. *Tomorrow*, she thought laying her head on the pillow.

The regular, metallic sound of the clock on her nightstand filled the quiet air, its endless chain of clicks pulling her toward the morning. She closed her eyes and turned onto her side, rolled back, punched the pillow, and buried her face.

I'm getting more exercise than sleep, she thought. She sat up and put her feet on the floor. She snapped on the bedside lamp, and rummaged through the stack of magazines piled under the nightstand. *Choose something dull, Kay.*

She pulled out an old *Time* magazine and flipped the pages without reading them, letting the pictures show her the stories of crime, misery, and occasionally new heroes, basking in the light of fame.

But then she felt it more than she heard it. Or maybe

was it both? She dropped the magazine and leaned forward, waiting to feel or hear more. But there was nothing except the sound time makes as it passes.

Had it come from outside? She pulled on her jacket, walked to the back door, and stepped into her boots. *Probably a raccoon.* The back porch light cast eerie shadows out toward the barn, but nothing scuttled away when she walked down the steps and quickly circled from the porch to the barn and back. *Maybe the front then?* Buster looked up from his cushion at the sudden brightness when the yellow light flooded the front porch.

"Sorry, old boy. False alarm." She turned off the light and locked up again. "Let's make another stab at sleeping."

At her door she paused. Still, there'd been something, she knew it. Kay walked down the hall to Shawna's door and listened. She tapped softly, and then stepped into the dark room.

The rumpled bed was empty.

Shawna lay sprawled on the floor.

Chapter 44

Shawna

"What's wrong with you?" Kay screams. She's standing next to me, but I hear her from very far away. Her face becomes many faces, falling over me like flower petals.

She pries open my hand. What do I have that she wants? Whatever it is, she's got it now. I search for my favorite memory—that motel somewhere, the woman with the long red braid, the spoon, the ice cream. How come Kay doesn't have a braid? Or ice cream?

She grabs me by the back of the neck, takes my hand and pulls me onto my feet, hauling me across the floor until I feel the cool bathroom tiles.

I think I'm laughing. Maybe it's because she grabs the chickens in the same way, takes them to "the block," and chops off their heads. *Is Kay going to chop off my head?*

"Stick your finger down your throat!" she yells. "Either you do it, or I will!"

"I . . . can—'t find . . ." I know what I want to say, but when I try, the words come out slushy.

My head is sinking toward the toilet bowl. I'm going to drown in it. But I feel Kay's hand tighten on my neck. It's strong and rough, and she's shaking me so much, my eyes seem to roll around in my head.

My mouth gapes and I feel her finger at the back of my throat. I gag, and up comes a wave of vomit. Chunks of pills spill into the water. Then there's more. I become the Niagara Falls of pill vomit for what seems like forever and ever.

Kay flushes the toilet. And when I throw up again, it's smelly and slimy, but there are no more white lumps.

Kay lets go and I slide down the wall to squat on the floor.

"Here." Kay shoves a damp towel into my hands. "Wipe your face."

She drags me to my feet and props me onto the toilet seat cover.

I hear the back door open and close, and then it's quiet. I'm alone. I'm still alive, my face buried in a towel that smells like vomit.

U

Kay dashed from the house to Kenny's trailer. But the distance seemed greater than ever before. Would she reach him in time? Why couldn't she move faster? Maybe Shawna was hurting herself again at this very moment. Kay's nightmare was coming to life.

A high-speed train whipped around a bend in the

tracks. The oncoming engine with its beam stretched out into the darkness, silhouetted Nic, standing, waiting, waving to her without seeing the train behind him.

Run, her brain screamed, but her feet were caught between metal rails, and she couldn't lift them. The train came nearer and nearer until it washed Nic away in its white light.

"Kenny!" she shouted and pounded on his door. The door flew open. "Grab your bag. It's Shawna. She's taken something. I made her throw up, but . . ."

Kenny was already running toward the house, his bag flapping at his side. "Where is she?" he shouted over his shoulder.

"The bathroom," she managed to say; then she leaned against the side of his trailer for a moment and wrapped her arms tightly around herself. *I couldn't save Nic*, she thought. *Please let me save Shawna.*

U

I hear Kenny's voice before I hear his footsteps on the back steps. The door swings open, and his boots clomp through the house until he's standing over me. He pulls my eyelids up, then puts his fingers around my wrist. He wraps something around my arm until I can feel my pulse thud against the tight band.

"What do you think?" Kay's voice is tense.

"Vitals are good. I think you got most of it out of her.

Let's get something into her stomach to soak up whatever's left. Come on, Missy. No more tossing your cookies tonight." He has me around the waist and I stumble down the hall with him until he drops me onto the living room couch.

A kitchen cabinet opens and closes, then the refrigerator door. The familiar sound of Kay's sturdy boots strides back to me. *That's a first. She didn't take off her boots. Neither did Kenny. They broke the boot rule! I made Kay Stone and Kenny Fargo break a house rule.* I didn't expect that.

"Eat these," she says.

I pull the towel down and look up.

"I don't think I . . ."

"Eat," Kenny says.

I take the crackers and chew on one very slowly, sure that it will come right back up all over me. It doesn't. Kay pushes a glass of milk into my hand, and I take a small sip. But the milk tastes like liquid chalk. I burp and hold the towel over my mouth. My throat burns like it's filled with hot acid, but still nothing comes up. I hold the glass out for Kay to take, but she pushes it back toward my mouth.

Stubborn old woman.

I take another sip, and work on keeping my head from turning itself inside out so everything around me will stop stretching like elastic. I concentrate on the coffee table in front of me. It should be a tidy square, but at the moment it snakes this way and that, like it's on the way out the door.

231

Chapter 45

Shawna

I must have fallen asleep after Kenny and Kay forced more crackers and milk into me. I wake up on the couch under one of Kay's afghans, with crumbs in the corners of my mouth and my brain kicking the back of my eyeballs.

Kay sits in her chair, drinking coffee and watching me. "Dr. Lubell said you'd feel very thirsty and probably shaky. Was she right?"

I try sitting up but give it up as a bad plan. Instead I stretch out with my eyes closed against the morning light.

"I guess she was."

A few minutes later, I feel a cool cloth on my forehead and Kay's fingers on my wrist. "See if you can sit up now. I'll get you some water."

I take my time and ease back against the pillows that Kay props behind me.

My head wobbles like one of those plates on a stick that jugglers twirl around, but with her hand to steady me, I manage to gulp down a glass of water before I fall asleep again.

The next time I open my eyes, the sun is shining on the back of the house. The porch, which I can see from the couch, is shaded. That means it's late afternoon.

My head isn't pounding and I don't feel like I'm about to hurl anymore, so I decide to test my legs. They don't buckle under me, and I can walk. Good thing, too, because I have to pee. I shuffle across the room and down the hall.

The bathroom mirror's afternoon feature is a horror show: matted hair, puffy eyes, skin that wintered under a rock. If I had died last night, I wouldn't be pretty on the slab today. And I always thought I'd make a very pretty dead person.

I splash water on my face and run my wet hands through my hair.

"Tell me again about the picture I had in my mind last night," I say to the face that looks more like Monster's than Shawna's. I was a sleeping beauty surrounded by pink satin. Marta, huge tears draining to her chin, leaned over to say good-bye. Deirdre, her bumpy nose red from crying, stared down at me, and Deanna of the two N's stood next to her, apologizing, too late, for being such a bitch. Casey stayed the longest and kissed me so softly that his lips were like moth wings on my forehead. The last to lean over me was Kay, with Kenny beside her. "I'm so sorry, Shawna," they said together, like one person speaking. *Wasn't there more? I just can't remember.*

I squeeze a glob of toothpaste onto my brush and attack the fur on my teeth, but I need to sit on the toilet while I brush. My legs are not ready to hold me upright for long.

233

What else don't I remember about last night? It was important. But not important enough, I guess.

When I come out of the bathroom, Kay is leaning against the wall, like she's waiting for her turn in a ladies' room line in a theater.

"You going to guard me twenty-four seven?" I ask.

"For a while. Until we can arrange to see Dr. Lubell again. But we have some decisions to make. Both of us." She takes my arm. "Come on. I've got soup on the table."

The soup's hot and good, and I'm hungry, even if my stomach is still sour. "I'm not going to school on Monday, right?"

"We'll talk to the therapist first. The appointment's at ten." She clears the table and sits down again across from me.

"So, what in the h—" Kay shakes her head like she has to erase that line and start again. "What were you thinking, taking those pills?"

I want to explain, but how do I explain Monster? I don't understand him. Monster used to hang out with me. He left after the lady with the single red braid came to stay and feed me ice cream, and laugh with me when Mom was gone and I was scared. About a year ago, when I was fifteen, Monster came back. Only he wasn't little and fun like before.

I was almost asleep when he swam up through the sheets, wrapped long wormy fingers around both my ankles and pulled until I was sure I'd disappear under the bed. At the moment my head was about to go under, he let go of me, and I curled myself into a tight fist, holding onto my knees.

The next time Monster came, he promised to help me if only I'd do one thing for him.

"What?"

"You know. It'll be our secret." And he whispered in my ear.

"No. It'll hurt."

"Only a little," he said. "And then you'll feel good."

He promised to help and I believed him. So I found one of Dylan's razor blades in the bathroom. At first I didn't like the feeling of the blade slicing across my ankle, but I grew to appreciate its cold thinness. It took me away from Mom and her Dylans, Randys and Jakes, from Tuan's snaky looks, and the greasy takeout boxes piled in the sink. For that moment of cutting, I didn't feel anything except the icy red line.

From then on, whenever I got the shakes and felt the touch of Monster's fingers, I'd slip Mr. Sharp from under my mattress and draw him across my skin—in places only I would see. And never too deep, just enough to stop being scared for a while. At least for that moment, I could control something.

"If I tell you, you'll think I'm nuts," I say to Kay, who never backs down from anything.

"Try me."

"Can I wait until my stomach isn't up here?" I point to my chest. I'm thinking I shouldn't have eaten.

"No."

See? She's stubborn. So I tell her about Monster, about the cutting, and how, as weird as it sounds to say so, it helps. "The shakes leave when I draw the line across my ankle. For just that minute, I'm in charge of my life. Jackie's gone. Tuan's apartment fades. Even Las Vegas goes dark and quiet."

"But here?" Her voice is just above a whisper.

I have to think, so I close my eyes and focus on her question. I see the house and barn, Kenny, Casey with the gray, Magic waiting at the fence, Kay with her mug of coffee Sunday mornings. Then there's Marta and school and—I open my eyes and look up at her.

"I don't know. Maybe it's what I brought with me. Monsters travel, I guess." When I finish, she doesn't say anything for a while, so my stomach has some time to go back to its normal business.

"So why the pills this time? Are you ratcheting up to really destroy yourself? You really want to leave me with your suicide as your good-bye?"

I know better than to shrug, so I answer her straight. "Yes. You never wanted me here in the first place."

Her knuckles, laced into a single tight fist, turn white. Her eyes stay fixed on me as she speaks in that slow way she has when she's had it with me.

"And you came to that conclusion all by yourself, did you?"

"No. Not all by myself. Jackie said so." I shouldn't have mentioned Jackie. Kay's face goes into a spasm, but the rest of her doesn't move and she's silent.

"You were the one who wanted to flush me. You wanted me gone a long time before I landed on your porch two months ago. You didn't want me, and my dad didn't either."

From the look on Kay's face, I expect she's going to explode and I'll be wearing bits of her. I've hit dead center on a sore spot. I consider backing away, leaving while I can before she blows. Instead, I stay put and keep my eyes locked on hers, waiting for her next move.

When Kay suddenly scrapes her chair back and stands up, I hold onto the table to keep from jumping out of reach. But she doesn't come at me like Jackie would. Instead, she goes to her office and returns holding a large leather book.

"You need to know about your father." She opens the book and drops it on the table in front of me.

"His name was Nicholas Stone, and he was a good son. He would have been a good father, but the service took him, so he was a good soldier instead. He died trying to save other people."

She's at my side and I can feel the heat of her, can almost feel her breath with each rise and fall of her chest. I clear my throat and take a chance on saying something else.

"Why do I need to know about him now?" I'm still half expecting my stomach to pop out of my mouth, with the way it's hopping around inside me.

"Because he was a lot braver than your mother or you, or . . . even I ever thought of being. He valued life. He didn't try to throw it away." Kay's voice has settled into a low and dangerous current. "And he never walked out on anybody . . . unless they forced him to go."

I know better than to open my mouth to tell her my mom's version of that story. Besides, I'm too tired to say much. So I look down at the album only to see a face so much like my own that I jerk back, letting the book fall flat onto the table.

"No question you're his daughter. I knew that at the bus station, or you'd never be living here now."

Chapter 46

Shawna

Kay gets up from the table. "When you're done going through the album, we'll talk. I'll tell you all about what happened, and you'll have to decide which version of the story to believe, Jackie's or mine."

She grabs her straw hat from the rack by the back door. "Can I trust you not to do anything else stupid for a while?"

"I'm out of pills."

"That's a dumb answer, Shawna. I want one that sounds intelligent, all right?"

"I'm too sick to kill myself today. Is that good enough?"

Kay turns and stomps down the steps.

I'm alone now, with my father looking up at me with dark, scolding eyes. Nicholas, age seventeen. The flat cap is pushed back on his head, its tassel dangles near his ear. He clutches a diploma in his hand.

I flip the pages backward. Nicholas, age twelve. He sits on a white horse, his smile spreading across his face;

C. Lee McKenzie

he squints at the lens. Nicholas, age ten. Tall, dark from the summer sun, he poses with a fishing pole and a string of fish he holds up for the camera—same smile, same squint.

Another page and another, going backward in time. Nicholas, Day One, 1970. Then Kay and Peter before Nicholas, 1968. Kay, her black hair pulled back gleaming under the sun, leaning over the porch of this same rough red house. A lean blond man sits beside her, his arm around her waist.

The yellow newspaper clipping is wedged between two empty pages. I open it and read:

April 10, 1991. Sweet River Native Lost in Desert Storm. Sergeant Nicholas Stone, Tank Commander of the Third Armored Division was killed this week while on patrol in the vicinity of the Safwan, Iraq refugee camp when he stepped on a land mine. He is survived by a wife and baby daughter—

"Baby daughter!" I inhale the words and hold them inside, not wanting them to vanish. I reread that line and run my finger underneath it, like I might lose my place.

—as well as his mother and father, long time Sweet River residents. Sergeant Stone attended Sweet River High School, where a memorial service is planned to honor his memory.

Mom told me my dad left because of me. She said he

ran off the week I was born and didn't tell her where he was going. She said he didn't want to see me. The clipping quivers in my hand and I have to put it down. I have to stop the shakes. I slam my hands onto the tabletop until my palms burn.

She lied! Damn her. Why?

I'm not shaking anymore. I place the heels of my hands over my eyes and press hard until the shadows dance behind my lids. I know why she lied. I wrote two reasons that first day in Mrs. Heady's English class. *There are times when a lie works a lot better than the truth.* And like Mark Twain wrote: *I would rather tell seven lies than make one explanation.*

Maybe my dad didn't run off because of me. Maybe he died thinking he'd return, make a family with Jackie and me. Or, here's an idea, he left her. She wouldn't want to explain that, would she? So now I have to sort out her fiction from the facts, and piece together what really happened before I was old enough to remember my own history, before she could reinvent it.

I turn back to the picture of my seventeen-year-old father.

"Would you have come back to me?"

I tuck the clipping back into its space, where it's been pressed all these years. After that, I find only empty pages. Kay's family ended that April day, someplace in a country I hear about all the time, without ever knowing its significance in my life.

I go back to the first pages of the photo album. These have the color and the feel of old newspapers left in the sun. When I let them fall page by page, they fan back the stale smell of used clothing stores or Tuan's back room full of poor people's discards.

Staring up at me are the faces of people who didn't find anything funny at that moment when they were photographed, or maybe never: Great-grandmother Stone, 1920. Grandfather Wescott, 1938.

My family tree is sprouting relatives faster than Buster sprouts fleas.

"Wonder what they'd say about old Jackie and me?" I close the book. "Who cares, anyway?"

"I do." Kay is at the door. "I'd hope they'd have good things to say."

"About Jackie, too?"

She sighs her way into her same chair. "Yes. Even about Jackie."

Kay studies her hands, like they might help her say what she needs to, then she looks at me. It's hard to read her, to see what's in her face. There are too many feelings stirred together, and I can tell she's sorting them out, deciding what and how to say what's in her head.

"Your mother was a sad child. Her father abandoned her and her mother when she was only five. Her mother was sick most of her life, so Jackie didn't have much except welfare checks and pity from people around here. We helped out when we could, but we didn't have much at that time, either. Her mother died. She went into foster care. She saw her chance to get out of Sweet River when she and Nic started dating at the end of his senior year."

So now I know the woman I was inside for nine months and what I was to her—a ticket out of Sweet River. "He knocked her up, right?"

"Shawna . . ." Kay puts her forearms on the table and leans forward. "Yes. She became pregnant, and Nic wouldn't abandon her."

"So—" I had this great question, and she didn't give me a chance to ask it.

"I didn't handle it right, Shawna. I drove Nic out of this house because I was too stupid to understand what kind of person he was. I helped make your life what it is. I'm responsible for all of it."

With lots to say, I opened my mouth.

Kay puts up a traffic-cop hand. "Wait!"

Her voice sounds like she'd cry if she could. I can tell she hated Nic's going into the army, that she blames herself for him going.

"I go over that last conversation with Nic every night of my life. I would take it all back, everything I said, if only I could."

She stops talking for a moment, then goes on.

"But—and this is the important part—because he was the kind of person he was, he would never abandon you. And that, Shawna, I promise you, is the absolute truth."

Chapter 47

Kay

Kay shook her head at Shawna's flip answers. *I'm out of pills, she says. Why can't she drop the hard crust? Just once, I'd like an answer that comes without grit.*

"I'm too sick to kill myself today. Is that good enough?"

"That's a dumb answer, Shawna. I want one that sounds intelligent, all right?"

How can she be so careless about what she's done? Kay grabbed her hat. *I'm not going to hear anything near what I want from this girl.* She turned and walked down the steps, punishing the boards under her boots.

Who was she mad at? Shawna? Herself? Monsters that came when you were about to take away the most precious thing you had? Shawna may not have thought that this grandmother understood the Monster but, one day . . . she'd tell her granddaughter how much she knew about him. And she knew a great deal.

Right now she had some other terrible business to finish, and Shawna needed time to get acquainted with her

244

family. Kay'd have to trust that her granddaughter was safe for the moment.

She made her way to the fence, climbed over, and walked to Floyd's shack. Victor's car was parked in back. The horses grazed on the dry pasture, and only the black one stopped to notice her passing.

Not the one I want, he seemed to say, before lowering his head and nipping again at the stubble.

Victor came from the house with a small cardboard box in his arms. "Afternoon, Kay. I planned to come over before I left."

"I was hoping you could put me in touch with the new owners, Vic. They may not want to sell me the property, but maybe they'll part with the horses, at least the black one."

"They called and said they couldn't get down for a couple of weeks and asked if I'd get them a caretaker until then. I hired Casey, that boy of yours." Victor set the box inside his truck and slammed the door.

Kay nodded. "He'll do a good job."

"Well, I'm done here. There's not much inside. Dad never did replace anything more than a mattress and stove. Didn't even have a refrigerator. He used an old camp cooler." He shook his head. "Can you imagine that?" He took off his hat and wiped the inside of the brim. When he put it on again, tears ran the length of his face.

The night his family home burned, he'd stood next to her, gripping her hand with both of his. She had pulled him from a sea of flames, and he'd clung to her like a lifeline.

Kay grabbed him and held him tight. Once again he was the shaking ten-year-old, unable to stop his tears.

"Some events twist around in us forever. That fire still carves out new edges inside me, and I can only imagine how it must torture you, Vic."

He stepped back and took her hands, much as he had that night, twenty-five years before. "Good-bye, Kay."

She watched him leave, heavy with the secret that even Floyd never knew. Only she and Nic knew the story of how that fire started.

She'd already turned to leave when Casey's truck stopped in almost the same spot that Victor had parked in moments before.

"Hear you have another job," Kay said when he climbed out of the cab.

"Yeah, for a couple of weeks, I guess. I'll still manage Sundays for you, Mrs. Stone."

She smiled. "I know you will." He was a reliable worker and a good person to have on the ranch. She liked his handling of the horses and she'd miss him when he left for college. "I hear you gave my granddaughter a ride home last night."

Casey's expression didn't change, but his eyes shifted toward the ground.

Something happened, Kay thought. And she needed to know what.

"Guess the sleepover at Marta's didn't go so well?" Maybe Casey'd give her something to go on, to help her understand what might have pushed Shawna—to do what she'd almost done.

"You got it. She stirred things up a lot . . . at least she did for me."

"Hmm. Anything I can do?" She wanted to dig a little deeper.

"No, Ma'am." He studied his boots. "I've got enough women doing things to and for me that I'm thinking I don't need any more." He looked up. "Sorry. I—"

"No need to say that." She walked to the fence. "But if you change your mind and need an older woman's help, let me know. And, Casey, when those new owners come, call me, okay? I'm thinking of buying those horses Floyd sold them."

He smiled. "Thought you'd give in and save those guys."

"It's Shawna who has me thinking that way."

"Yeah. I'd like to know what she says to the black one, but he's not telling me anything." He waved and went into the barn.

It was time to go back and check on Shawna. When Kay came up the back steps, Shawna was focused so intently on the photo album that she didn't look up when Kay opened the door.

"Wonder what they'd say about old Jackie and me?" Shawna closed the book. "Who cares, anyway?"

"I do. I'd hope they'd have good things to say," Kay said.

"About Jackie, too?"

The way she said her mother's name reminded Kay of a spike being driven into metal. She sagged into her chair. "Yes. Even about Jackie."

Time to tell all, Kay thought. I need to make it short and true, no hedging. Shawna would make a hell of a card player, because she watches people when they say or do anything, and she listens more than she talks. Good thing too. Her language is already spilling over into mine. I'm sprinkling hells and damns everywhere, and pretty soon, if I don't watch out, I'll be matching her one for one.

The story wasn't as hard to tell as she'd thought. Jackie's bad childhood. Her bad luck. Her good to excellent survival instincts that included Nic. There it was.

"He knocked her up, right?"

"Shawna . . ." What was the use? "Yes. She became pregnant, and Nic wouldn't abandon her."

The hardest part wasn't over. Kay had to tell the truth about her part if she was going to make Shawna believe the truth about her father.

She wanted to scream, *it was me! I did it. I pay for it every day of my life, and every night I relive that moment, and I can't ever make it up to you!* But she didn't scream. She didn't use those words. This wasn't about her. This was about Shawna and her father, Nic.

"He went into the service so he'd have a way to go to college when he got out. He wanted more than anything to give you a home and a decent life. I spoke to him just before he shipped out. I . . . was too late to stop him—he'd already enlisted. But—and this is the important part—because he was the kind of person he was, he would never abandon you. And that, Shawna, I promise you, is the absolute truth."

U

That night, even Kay's bones felt tired. Her arms and legs lay heavy against the sheets. Her head weighed enough to sink a dinghy. Shawna lay next to her, her breath steady and deep. She had been alone so long in this bed that Kay treasured the sound, and if it was possible, she would seal it inside a bottle to release later and hear again beside her.

The memories of yesterday perched in the front of her brain, vivid and haunting. But there was more, something at the base of her skull that wouldn't go away, something that just wouldn't come forward. She'd sleep and in the morning—*No, now!*

U

She was back in the kitchen, facing Nic and Jackie.

Where was Peter? At the window, silent.

He stared out at the barn, like he had nothing to do with the conversation. He really wasn't there; instead, he was riding on the trail, escaping, and she hadn't even picked up on it.

She'd been so angry and scared that her son was about to make the biggest mistake of his life, she hadn't thought about Peter. She didn't question why he remained silent, then and later.

Sixteen years to pick up on the fact that Peter was leaving before Nic ever came to you about Jackie, before he died in Iraq. Nicholas's death was the final blow to an already dead relationship. Finally, Peter couldn't ignore the corpse of their marriage anymore.

And I was the smart one in college!

Chapter 48

Shawna

The next morning when I open my eyes, I'm staring up at Kenny Fargo, who's got one of those doctor things dangling around his neck. "Morning, Missy. Let's get a listen to that heart of yours."

"I'm not a horse, in case you haven't noticed."

"Sounds like you're back to normal. We'll have a listen anyway." He sticks the plugs into his ears and puts the cold end on my chest. Then he holds my wrist and looks at his watch. "Yep. You'll live. Guess I won't have to take my black suit to the cleaners after all."

"I'd laugh if you'd say something funny."

"I'd laugh if you'd do something besides scare the bejibbers out of your grandmother. You try something like that again, I'll wallop you back to Vegas myself."

I'd like to punch him in the nose. "Don't I have a right to die if I want to? It's my life, damn it!"

"No, you don't have the right. Fact is, the law says we can put you someplace where you'll get your own personal shrink and a nice little room where you'll be safe—even from yourself. Did you know that, Missy?"

I don't see Kay until she's at the foot of the bed. "Actually, Shawna, if we involve the authorities, Dr. Lubell tells me we'll have tons of legal problems."

She sits on the bed. "Your mother is still your legal guardian. She has the final say about where you go or don't go, unless I try to gain custody. That's what I meant yesterday, about decisions we both have to make."

"You two don't need old doc anymore." Kenny snaps his bag shut and picks it up. "I'm going back to the barn where my patients are more congenial." Then he leaves us alone.

"I'm calling your mother this morning. What do you want me to say about all this?"

I shrug.

"I thought we'd passed the shrugging stage in our communication. Haven't we?"

"Don't tell her anything, okay?"

"I'm going to ask her to sign over legal guardianship to me. Do you agree on this?"

I study my lap.

"If you don't agree, I won't ask her. But then, even Dr. Lubell won't see us again. I . . . didn't quite tell her or the school the truth about everything."

I look up at Kay. "What truth are you talking about?"

"I said I was your legal guardian. It was easier to lie than to explain, but that was my mistake."

I gasp and she looks at me, confused for a moment.

"It was you," I say.

"I don't understand."

"You underlined all that stuff Mark Twain said in that

book. '*I would rather tell seven lies than make one explanation.*'" From her expression, I know I'm right. She
poured over *Pity is for the living, envy for the dead.* I study
her, and try to see past the creases at her mouth and eyes,
past the face I've come to know as Kay Stone, my grandmother.

"That was a long time ago," Kay says. "And I had
very different problems than now."

She looks away, like she's thinking about how to steer
the topic back where she wants it—to my mother and the
problems I've brought down on her head.

"Now, since all of this suicide business, the therapist
has to see documentation, something only your mother can
give me. Then the school will be next. So what's it going
to be? Shall I call Jackie and ask her to sign the papers
making me your legal guardian?"

I think about my choices, when that beautiful, horrible word pops up again, *di-lem-ma!* I can stay here with
Kay, curry horses, follow a zillion rules, give Marta Hip-
Hop lessons, and put another bump in Deirdre's nose when
she sticks it into my business.

Or I can go back to Mommie and another Tuan-apart-
ment life. I hold out my hands like a balancing scale.
Sweet River on my left: no freedom, lots of Sundays. Las
Vegas on my right: nothing but freedom, nothing but
Sweethearts.

It almost seems like a wash, that is, until I think about
Magic, until I remember the last part of my own Sleeping
Beauty funeral—the part I couldn't remember before.
Mom never came to look down at me. She never came to

say good-bye. But somebody else did. The woman with a single long red braid, tied with a velvet ribbon. The woman from when I was five, who floats in and out of memory.

U

At my dream funeral, she looked down on me . . . and she propped me on pillows and fed me ice cream with a small spoon and said she'd miss me.

U

I look up at Kay, remembering. "Ask her to sign me over."

Kay sighs—that same sigh that comes up from her boots, whenever I say something in a way she doesn't like to hear it.

"I'll ask," she says. "Now go get showered and dressed. I've already called the school and told them you wouldn't be there today. Once I talk to your mother, we may have a lot of things to do."

Chapter 49

Kay

In her office, Kay pulled out the wrinkled paper Shawna had left with Jackie's number written on it. She punched in the numbers and waited. If she asked Jackie like she would an ordinary human being, Jackie would never sign over legal custody. How was she going to get this woman to do what had to be done, what was in Shawna's best interest? How—

"Hello." Jackie's voice, heavy with sleep, came over the line.

"It's Kay. I need you to sign custody papers for Shawna so I can get medical coverage for her. Otherwise, I'll have to send you the bills. Which way do you want me to handle it?"

"What papers?" Jackie seemed to be struggling to make sense of Kay's question.

"I'm sending some papers for you to sign. If you don't, you'll have to pay Shawna's doctor bills."

"Is she sick?"

"No. But the school says I have to have insurance for

her, and since I'm not her legal guardian, I can't get it." Kay wondered if that were really true. "Will you sign the papers if I send them to you?"

"Papers? Sure."

"Where do I send them?" Kay asked, picking up her pen. She waited. "Jackie?" Had the woman gone back to sleep? "Hello?"

"Had to look outside."

Kay rolled her eyes and wrote down the address. The phone went dead as soon as she'd gotten everything except the ZIP Code. Was the woman drunk? High?

Kay looked at her watch. It was only eight-fifteen in the morning.

Chapter 50

Shawna

My room looks like a cleaning service came through it. Nothing's on the floor, the bed is smooth and tight at the edges. The curtains are pulled back and the windows are open, making the air inside as fresh as the October day beyond the screen. This isn't the room I remember from Saturday night. It's been flushed and scrubbed and disinfected.

I shower, dress, and dry my hair, and when I look in the mirror, I've changed from zombie back to dork. But the dorky girl looks better than I remember from the old Las Vegas days. "Hmm." *So Deirdre is jealous of me.* "Interesting."

"Are you ready, Shawna?" Kay calls down the hall.

For what? I wonder. I grab a sweatshirt and walk to her office. "I thought you said I wasn't going to school today."

"You're not. We've got an appointment with my lawyer. Your mother's agreed to give me legal custody, so we're going to get the papers ready and send them right away…" She comes from behind her desk. "…before she changes her mind."

I know Kay's right. Jackie changes her mind more than she changes her underwear, but ugh . . . another trip to Sacramento . . . in that truck . . . with my silent driver.

I'll go see Magic, give him his apple and his vitamin, which he missed yesterday. Just a minute with the old boy, and I'll be ready to take on Kay and her truck.

"Meet you at the truck," I say halfway out the office door, before Kay can tell me we don't have time.

I don't cut up the apple this time. I slice it in half, dump two vitamin pills into the palm of my hand, and run across the field to the fence.

"Magic!"

I climb the fence and throw my leg over the top like always and wait. "Magic!" I call again. "Where are you, you ornery old horse?"

I shield my eyes with both hands and scan the pasture. Not a horse in sight.

I jump to the ground, run to Floyd's barn, and rip open the doors.

Empty.

I try to keep my breathing steady, but I can't. I feel the same way I did the morning I found Mom's note and the ticket with Kay's name and number on the note. That cold numbness pours over me, finds its way into my stomach, and makes me sick.

I have to do something. I have to . . . *get my grandmother.*

I charge back across the field and hurdle the fence,

run to the house, up the back steps and through the kitchen door, letting it bang closed behind me. I run down the hall to Kay's office. "Magic's gone!"

She stands up from her desk and comes to me. "Magic?"

"My . . . Floyd's black horse." I'm trying not to shriek.

"Magic," Kay repeats. "Did you check Floyd's barn?"

"Yes. He's not there." Saying that makes my stomach knot up tighter than before. "There's not one horse anywhere out there."

"Come on. Let's ask Kenny if he knows what's going on."

I jog behind Kay to the barn, where we find Kenny in the tack room.

"Floyd's horses," Kay says, "they're gone."

Kenny looks at her like he's not heard what she said. "Thought I saw something going on there this morning. Strange truck. Just reckoned it was the new people, comin' to check out the property."

"Did they have a horse trailer?" Kay asks.

"Yep. But I didn't stay to watch what was happening." Kenny nods toward me. "Had little Missy here to check on."

"How about Casey? Was he around?"

"He was driving into Floyd's when I came out of the house, but I didn't see him after that. Figured he did his chores, then went to school." Kenny walks outside and looks across at Floyd's. He rubs his chin like that might make him remember more about what he saw earlier. "Dang. Shoulda' gone over when I saw that truck . . . that truck . . ." He faces us. "It had Texas plates."

"No!" I cup my hands over my ears. I'm choking. I feel like something has me by the throat and is pressing the life out of me. The fingers are tight and growing tighter.

Sharp pins of light dance across Kay's face. The barn, Kenny, Floyd's shack across the field—all whirl around like a crazy Ferris wheel. Or maybe it's me. I'm whirling and everything else is fixed.

Then dynamite's exploding in my head. Bam! Bam! Fingers slip away, and tears rush down my face. I don't care if Kay sees me crying. I don't care if Kenny sees me either.

Kay grabs my shoulders and pulls me to face her. "I'm not promising anything, but if we can get Magic back . . .?"

She doesn't finish her question, but I know what she's asking. Will I be Shawna Stone for real? Her granddaughter? Marta's friend? The AP student? There are a lot of questions inside the real one: *Will I change?*

I step away, out of Kay's reach and look into her eyes. I'm searching to see if they'll say she'd just as soon buy my ticket back to Vegas and be done with me. That she doesn't want to have to stand suicide watch every day and night. That being my legal guardian isn't how she wants to spend the rest of her life. That she's tired of my weird Monster fantasy, my foul mouth. That I'm a disappointment to her. I expect something like that to be there, staring back at me.

But it's not. What's staring back are eyes that say *I understand how you feel, losing something you love. I love you and I don't want to lose you, too.*

I feel a lot of things right now. I feel scared for Magic.

I feel scared for me, and I have this new, strangled feeling in my chest. Something I've never had before. Then I hear my own voice rising out of that strangled mess. "I will love him. I will love him. I will love him."

I can't believe it—now, Kay is crying. Big fat tears roll to her chin, and she doesn't bother to brush them off. "Oh, Shawna," she says. "I love you so much."

She pulls me to her and we cling to each other, like we'll fall into an ocean and drown if either one lets go.

"Mrs. Stone!" It's Casey's voice.

I look up and he's running toward us around the back side of the house.

"They've got Floyd's horses." He's waving a paper in his hand.

"Who has them?" Kay asks.

Casey hands her the paper. "When I came to check on them this morning, I found this pinned to the barn door."

Kay glances at the paper. "It's a bill of sale . . . Mesa Verde Enterprises, Pecos, Texas."

"I tried to catch up with them and stop them, but they had too much of a head start. I thought you ought to know they're heading down Highway 99." Casey looks at me. "I'm really sorry, Shawna."

There's no anger in his face, no "it serves you right" in his voice. He would have stopped the truck and brought Magic back to me because he's always known I had that black horse tucked under my heart. I want to tell him he was right from the beginning. I want to say something to let him know I'm sorry, too . . . for a lot of things.

261

"Mrs. Stone," he says, handing Kay his truck keys, "take my truck. It's faster."

"Thank you, Casey." Kay turns to Kenny. "Hitch up the trailer. Most truckers stop at Santa Nella, so I'm betting these guys will too. I'll go ahead and try to stop them. We can keep in touch by cell."

"You plannin' to hijack that truck?" Kenny asks.

"I'm planning on saving those horses. If it takes hijacking, so be it." Kay grabs my arm. "Go in the house and get the truck keys for Kenny." She pushes me toward the house. "They're on the kitchen table. Get going or Magic's going to be at the other end of the state."

I take the steps by twos, snatch the keys, and run back outside. I toss the keys to Casey, who grabs them and then takes my hand. "When we get Magic back to the ranch, let's talk, okay? And I mean talk—not fight."

I manage a nod and that seems to be the right thing, because now Casey smiles and wipes a tear that's trickling to my chin. Before I make it around the side of the house to Casey's truck, he and Kenny are maneuvering the horse trailer into place to hook it up.

Kay has the passenger door open, and is already behind the wheel. She's disconnecting from a call on her cell.

"Yes, cancel this afternoon's meeting. I'll be in first thing in the morning about the custody papers."

I climb inside and buckle up my seat belt—*another first*, I think. *I'm going over to a whole other side of the world.*

Kay slides the gears into reverse, whips around, and spins the wheels over the gravel. The ride down the road is the worst, and I'm clinging for my life to the door, the dash, the seat. At the "T" where she has to turn left, she doesn't stop to look both ways. She is a rule breaker today, and, at this moment, I see the girl she used to be—reckless, full of energy, strong-minded.

She hangs a right at the next corner, and shoots across two lanes of traffic to make a quick left onto the highway. I've thought about dying so many times, that it's a surprise not to want to die now. If I do, so will Magic, and I want him to live very much.

A tight, hard feeling squeezes the breath out of me. I'm sad and excited and scared, all at the same time. But there are no more shakes. I'm steady inside, like I haven't been since I was five. Since the woman I knew only a little while, in some motel I can't remember, came to me.

She wore her hair in a single long red braid, and propped me up on pillows and fed me ice cream, and let me lick the spoon . . .

And she laughed and I laughed—

Epilogue

From the porch I watch Casey's truck turn onto Kay's *arroyo seco* and make the rodeo ride over those gullies and mounds that I've learned to love—the way home.

Kenny calls it "shock absorber hell" before he spits and gets out the shovel to fill in the worst holes. Kay used to vow to fix it soon, one day, next year. But that was before last week, when she spent the money set aside to do the roadwork. Now those repairs will have to wait.

Tucked behind other thoughts, I have a plan to help out with expenses—a job in the summer, maybe at Rural Supply—if Max will trust me with the cash register. If not, I can always wait tables at the café in Sweet River. I'll find a way to help smooth out at least one road for Kay.

Casey pulls to a stop and gets out of his truck, October dust rising around him. He waves and walks toward me, holding up a bag in one hand. "Brought your order."

I walk down the steps to meet him. "Thanks."

"No problem. Max's was on my way." His hand brushes mine when he gives me the bag, and I freeze that moment, to save it for later.

I'm freezing moments a lot now, ever since last week's high-speed chase down Highway 99. My feelings are so different—so alive, I guess I have to say—and I need to go over them a few times, to get used to what it's like to touch people and not get the shakes. Get used to what it's like to talk to somebody—you know, in real conversations. Me—Shawna Stone—saying things, and listening to what people say back.

Casey and I walk to the barn. I let him go a little ahead and enjoy the view of his jeans again. He turns to smile over his shoulder. "So how are your patients doing, Dr. Stone?"

"Better."

I open the bottle of pills Casey picked up at Rural Supply, grab a tin pan from the bench near the door, and add water. Then I mash three pills into gruel.

"Want me to do the other two?" he asks.

"Sure. Their pans are in front of the stalls." I hand him the bottle and enter the hazy light of the barn, the world of straw, droning flies, and soft equine noises.

There you are, I hear from the stall at the end, and my heart fills up with what I know must be flowers. Big yellow ones.

What? I just saw you this morning. You want me around twenty-four seven?

He eyes me. *And your sense of humor has improved.*

No. You're just beginning to appreciate it.

You're probably right, Shawna.

Magic scarfs down his pills while I stand, leaning against his side, soaking in his warmth and his smell, and the wonderful size of him.

He swings his head and nudges me. *No apple?*

I reach into my pocket and pull out the package of slices. *You are one demanding horse!*

I'm making up for lost time. He snuffles the apple from my palm, and I wish I could give him a hundred apples, just so I could feel him do that over and over.

So am I, Magic. So am I.

Acknowledgments

Many thanks to everyone who directly or indirectly let Shawna's story come to the page:

Evelyn Fazio, who gave my first novel a chance;

Mary PB, who listened to the idea many times while we hiked;

The Garret writers: Lisa Madigan, Melissa Higgins, and Heather Strum, who slogged through the early drafts;

Nan Merino, Neesha Meminger, and Sandra Alonzo, who were patient and insightful readers;

And Jim, my husband, who answered the door and took my phone messages, then didn't complain when dinner was late.

7-12-13

AUG 0 1 2013